Gargoylz

Spring Mayhem!

Gargoylz: grotesque stone
creatures found on old
buildings, spouting rainwater
from the guttering.
Sometimes seen causing
mischief and mayhem
before scampering away
over rooftops.

Read all the Gargoylz adventures!

Gargoylz

Spring Mayhem!

Burchett & Vogler

illustrated by Leighton Noyes

RED FOX

GARGOYLZ SPRING MAYHEM

A RED FOX BOOK 978 1 849 41444 9

First published in Great Britain by Red Fox, an imprint of Random House Children's Books
A Random House Group Company

This edition published 2011
Collection copyright © Random House Children's Books, 2011

1 3 5 7 9 10 8 6 4 2

Toby Turns Up is taken from **GARGOYLZ ON THE LOOSE!** First published in Great Britain by Red Fox, 2009

Kitten Caper is taken from **GARGOYLZ GET UP TO MISCHIEF** First published in Great Britain by Red Fox, 2009

Fossil Fun is taken from **GARGOYLZ TAKE A TRIP** First published in Great Britain by Red Fox, 2009

Rocket Ride is taken from **GARGOYLZ MAGIC AT THE MUSEUM** First published in Great Britain by Red Fox, 2010

Midnight Feast Fun is taken from **GARGOYLZ AT A MIDNIGHT FEAST** First published in Great Britain by Red Fox, 2009

Man Overboard is taken from **GARGOYLZ MAKE A SPLASH** First published in Great Britain by Red Fox, 2010

Skeleton Scare is taken from **GARGOYLZ HAVE FUN AT THE FAIR** First published in Great Britain by Red Fox, 2010

Pink Princess Peril! is taken from **GARGOYLZ GO TO A PARTY** First published in Great Britain by Red Fox, 2010

Holiday Plans is taken from **GARGOYLZ ON THE GO** First published in Great Britain by Red Fox, 2010

Castle Chaos is taken from **GARGOYLZ RIDE TO THE RESCUE** First published in Great Britain by Red Fox, 2010

Series created and developed by Amber Caravéo

The Random House Group Limited supports The Forest Stewardship Council (FSC),
the leading international forest certification organisation. All our titles that are printed on Greenpeace
approved FSC certified paper carry the FSC logo. Our paper procurement policy can be found at
www.rbooks.co.uk/environment.

Set in Bembo Schoolbook

Red Fox Books are published by Random House Children's Books,
61–63 Uxbridge Road, London W5 5SA

www.kidsatrandomhouse.co.uk
www.rbooks.co.uk

Addresses for companies within The Random House Group Limited can be found at:
www.randomhouse.co.uk/offices.htm

THE RANDOM HOUSE GROUP Limited Reg. No. 954009

A CIP catalogue record for this book is available from the British Library.

Printed and bound in Great Britain by CPI Bookmarque, Croydon, CR0 4TD

With special thanks to Jan and Sara,
for bringing the Gargoylz to life so beautifully.

Oldacre Primary School

garden

staff car park

staffroom

playing field

St Mark's Church

playground

School Report - Max Black

Days absent: 0

Days late: 0

Max is never afraid to make a contribution to history lessons. His demonstration of a battering ram using a broom and a bucket was very realistic, although the resulting hole in the classroom door was not ideal.

I worry that Max only seems to play with Ben Neal, but he assures me he has a lot of friends at the local church.

Class teacher - Miss Deirdre Bleet

Max Black's behaviour this term has been outrageous. He has repeatedly broken school rule number 739: boys must not tell 'knock knock' jokes in assembly. He is still playing pranks with Ben Neal. Mrs Pumpkin is absent again after the exploding paint pot incident. And Mrs Simmer, the head dinner lady, says the mincing machine has never been the same since he fed his maths test into it.

Head teacher - Hagatha Hogsbottom (Mrs)

School Report - Ben Neal

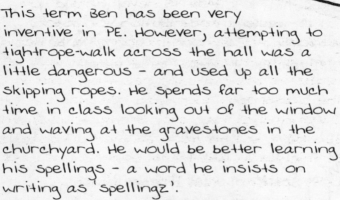

Days absent: 0
Days late: 0

This term Ben has been very inventive in PE. However, attempting to tightrope-walk across the hall was a little dangerous – and used up all the skipping ropes. He spends far too much time in class looking out of the window and waving at the gravestones in the churchyard. He would be better learning his spellings – a word he insists on writing as 'spellingz'.

Class teacher - Miss Deirdre Bleet

Ben Neal is always polite, but I am deeply concerned about his rucksack. It often looks very full – and not with school books, I am certain. It has sometimes been seen to wriggle and squirm. I suspect that he is keeping a pet in there. If so, it is outrageous and there will be trouble.

Head teacher - Hagatha Hogsbottom (Mrs)

Meet the Gargoylz!

Full name: Tobias the Third

Known as: Toby

Special Power: Flying

Likes: All kinds of pranks and mischief - especially playing jokes on the vicar

Dislikes: Mrs Hogsbottom, garden gnomes

Full name: Barnabas

Known as: Barney

Special Power: Making big stinks!

Likes: Cookiez

Dislikes: Being surprised by humanz

Name: Eli

Special Power: Turning into a grass snake

Likes: Sssports Day, Ssslithering

Full name: Bartholomew

Known as: Bart

Special Power: Burping spiders

Likes: Being grumpy

Dislikes: Being told to cheer up

Full name: Theophilus

Known as: Theo

Special Power: Turning into a ferocious tiger (well, tabby kitten!)

Likes: Sunny spots and cosy places

Dislikes: Rain

Full name: Zackary

Known as: Zack

Special Power: Making himself invisible to humanz

Likes: Bouncing around, eating bramblz, thistlz, and anything with pricklz!

Dislikes: Keeping still

Full name: Nebuchadnezzar
Known as: Neb
Special Power: Changing colour
to match his background
Likes: Snorkelling
Dislikes: Anyone treading on his tail

Name: Azzan
Special Power: Breathing fire
Likes: Surprises
Dislikes: Smoke going up his
nose and making him sneeze

Full name: Abel
Special Power: Turning into a tree
Likes: Funny puns and word jokes
Dislikes: Dogs weeing up
against him

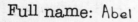

Name: Ruben
Special Power: Can go anywhere
in the world in a blink of an eye
Likes: Mrs Santa's baking
Dislikes: Delivering Christmas presents
to houses where there aren't any snackz
for Santa and his reindeer

Full name: Jehieli
Known as: Jelly
Special Power: Turning to jelly
Likes: Having friendz to play with
Dislikes: Bulliez and spoilsports

Name: Ira
Special Power: Making it rain
Likes: Making humanz walk the plank
Dislikes: Being bored

Name: Cyrus
Special Power: Singing lullabies
to send humanz to sleep
Likes: Fun dayz out
Dislikes: Snoring

Name: Rufus
Special Power: Turning into
a skeleton
Likes: Playing spooky tricks
Dislikes: Squeezing into
small spaces

Contents

Toby Turns Up

Max Black zoomed out of his front door.
He was playing his usual game on the
way to school. He was a nine-year-old
secret agent, speeding along in his super-
powered spy plane.

"MAX!"

He skidded to a halt,
trainers smoking. His
mum was standing in the
front garden.

"You've forgotten your
school bag again!" she called,
holding it out.

1

Max ran back and snatched it up.

"Did you brush your hair this morning?" demanded his mother.

"Yes, Mum." Of course he hadn't. He'd lost his brush down the toilet months ago. His dark brown hair stuck up all over the place and that was how he liked it.

Max set off along the pavement again. There was a boy ahead of him dribbling a football. Max activated his spy radar to check him out: blond hair, blue eyes, big grin, nine and a quarter years old.

He knew what that meant. It was Ben
Neal, codename: Best Friend.

Max sneaked up behind him. "Agent
Black ready for action," he hissed in
Ben's ear.

Ben grinned and passed the ball to
Max's feet. "New spy mission," he yelled,
running ahead. "Get football to school at
top speed."

They were soon at the gates. Max
looked up at Oldacre Primary School,
sandwiched between the ancient stone
church and the post office.

"Another day of torture," he groaned.

"Bell's not rung yet," said Ben. "Let's practise some nifty football skills."

"You're on," said Max as they ran through the playground. His spy radar homed in on someone: pale, skinny, face like a weasel. Max knew what that meant. It was Enemy Agent Lucinda Tellingly, codename: Bossy Boots. "Bet you can't lob the ball right over Lucinda's head."

"That'll be hard," said Ben. "She's got the biggest head in the world!"

Lucinda was standing near the netball hoop. Ben placed the ball carefully on the ground and took three steps back.

"Watch," he said. "Straight over her head and through the hoop."

4

Wham! Up went the ball. Down it came – **thump!** – right on top of Lucinda's ponytail. It bounced off sideways and landed on the low flat roof over the staffroom.

"Now look what you've done, Lucinda," moaned Ben, peering up at the ball. "It's stuck."

"Good!" snapped Lucinda. "I hope you never get it back." Lucinda didn't like Max and Ben – the boys had no idea why.

Just then, the bell rang for the beginning of school and Lucinda stomped off, tidying her ponytail.

"How am I going to get my ball down?" sighed Ben, ignoring the bell.

"We could try a fishing rod with glue on the end," suggested Max.

Ben's eyes lit up. "Brilliant plan, Agent Black." Then he frowned. "There's just one tiny problem – we don't have a fishing rod."

"Then we'll have to get onto the roof," said Max. "And I know how. We'll climb

up on that skip in the teachers' car park."

The skip was full of old furniture. Using a bookcase as a ladder, the boys were soon up on the staffroom roof.

Suddenly there was a skittering, scrabbling noise behind them. They whirled round.

Their eyes nearly popped out of their heads. A very peculiar creature was bounding towards them. It was the size of a puppy and it scampered along on all four paws. It had a monkey face with long pointy ears and golden eyes that glinted in the sunshine. Its skin looked exactly like the stone on the church next door.

Leafy wings sprouted from its back and its dragon-like tail wagged merrily.

The creature skidded to a halt, squatted on its hind legs and gave Max and Ben a huge grin.

"I think it's a gargoyle!" whispered Max.

"Do you mean one of those stone things on the church?" asked Ben.

"Yes," said Max. "They hang under the gutters and spout rainwater."

"But it can't be a gargoyle," Ben objected. "Gargoyles are just statues. They're not alive."

"This one is," said Max, staring.

"Greetingz," said the gargoyle merrily. His voice was a mixture between a growl and a purr – like a sort of dog-cat. "I'm Tobias the Third. You can call me Toby. I live on the church porch." He put his head on one side and peered at them. "Spluttering gutterz!" he chortled. "Are you school gargoylz? You're the ugliest ones I've ever seen."

"We're not gargoyles," Max told him.

Toby's impish face creased up in a
frown. "Of course you're
gargoylz!" he said.
"You were climbing
on the roof and
making mischief. Only
gargoylz do that." He
gave Max's arm a
pinch. "Your stone is
a bit flabby though."

"We're not made
of stone," Ben explained.

"We're boys. I'm Ben and this
is Max."

Toby looked
horrified. "You mean
you're humanz?
But humanz aren't
supposed to know that
gargoylz are alive!

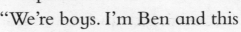

9

What am I going to do?" He began to wail and bite his claws.

"We won't tell anyone about you," Max shouted above the noise. "We promise, don't we, Ben?"

"I promise never to tell a soul that gargoylz are alive," Ben said solemnly. He picked up his football. "Cross my heart and may I never play with this again if I do."

Toby perked up immediately. "Glad we got that sorted out," he purred.

A booming voice suddenly rose from below. "What are you boys doing?"

Toby looked startled. "Freeze!" he whispered. He squatted on his haunches, put on a frozen, wide-mouthed snarl and kept absolutely still. Now he looked just like the gargoyles on the church.

Max peered cautiously over the guttering. He activated his spy radar: grey hair, beaky nose, steam coming out of ears. He knew what that meant.

It was Enemy Agent
Mrs Hogsbottom,
commonly known
as Mrs Hogsbum,
codename: Evil
Head Teacher.

"Outrageous!" she
screeched at them.
"Get down at once!"

Max and Ben got down.

"I might have known it would be you
two," the head teacher said, studying
them with her laser vision. "If there's any
trouble, Max Black and Ben Neal are
always behind it! I have not forgotten your
spaghetti forest in the teachers' toilet last
week. Poor Mr Widget still turns pale at
the mention of pasta."

"But we were just trying to brighten
the place up a bit—" Ben protested.

"Silence!" snapped Mrs Hogsbottom.
"The school bell has rung and where do I

find you? Running about on the roof."

"We weren't running, miss," Max tried to explain. "We—"

"No arguing!" ordered Mrs Hogsbottom fiercely. "School rule number fifty-six: children must not argue."

Ben put on his special wide-eyed innocent face. It always worked on the dinner ladies, who gave him extra sausages. It never worked on Mrs Hogsbum. Her bony fingers shot out and snatched the football from him.

"But—" began Max.

"Get to your classroom at once!" snapped the head teacher.

"When can I have my—?" began Ben.

"You can have your football back at the end of the week," snarled Mrs Hogsbum as she stormed off, "and not before!"

"How ungrateful!" fumed Max.
"Especially when we saved the caretaker
all the trouble of having to fetch it for us."
He looked up at the roof. "Toby? Are you
still there?"

There was a scrabbling sound and then
the gargoyle's chirpy little face appeared
over the edge of the gutter. "Glad that ugly
monster's gone," he said.

"She's worse than a monster," Max
told him. "Monsters run away when they
see *her*."

"And now she's got my football,"
grumbled Ben. "I bet that's the last I'll see
of it."

"She might burst it with her horrible

14

sharp nose," said Max.
"Or flatten it under
a pile of maths books,"

said Ben.
"Or cut
it into tiny
pieces and
boil it up in her
cauldron," Max added.

"I know what will
cheer you up," grinned
Toby. "I'll show you
how I can fly. It's my
special power."

"Awesome!" said Ben,
football forgotten.

But before Toby
could move, Mrs
Hogsbottom's head

popped out of the staffroom window like
a fearsome jack-in-the-box. "Off to class!"
she bellowed. "IMMEDIATELY!"

The boys scampered for the door.
Max looked back to wave at Toby, but
the gargoyle had gone.

"Did you see Toby's wings?" whispered
Max as he and Ben bent over their class
maths test. "I can't wait to see him fly."

"And he talked about making mischief,"
said Ben. "He's our sort of gargoyle!"

"I've just had a brilliant idea," declared
Max. "We must get to the girls' loo – now."

Ben looked horrified. "You call that a
brilliant idea? I wouldn't be seen dead in
that stinky place. It's all clean and flowery!"

"True," Max agreed. "But if you look
out of one of the windows up there, you
can see the staffroom roof. We might spot
Toby again."

"Good thinking, Agent Black," said Ben.

"That *is* a brilliant idea. There's just one problem – we need to come up with a way to get out of here."

"Max and Ben!" snapped a voice behind them.

Max's spy radar told him what that meant: short and dumpy, limp brown hair, silly half-moon glasses. It was Enemy Agent Miss Bleet, codename: Wimpy Teacher.

"Wasting time chatting, are we?" sighed Miss Bleet. She always sounded tired when she spoke to Max and Ben. Max thought she should go to bed earlier. "Ben, go and sit with Poppy," she went on. "Max, stay where you are. Then you might both do some work."

"See you in the girls' loos," Max hissed as Ben

SPY FILE:

code name: wimpy Teacher

pushed his
chair back noisily.
Max chewed his
pencil. He was just
wondering how to escape
when a paper aeroplane
sailed past Miss Bleet, who nearly fell into
the wastepaper bin in fright. The missile
banked and turned and hit Max on the
ear. He picked it up. It was Ben's maths
test – beautifully folded.

"Ben Neal!" quavered their teacher.
"Go and stand outside in the corridor."

Max was impressed. Who'd have
thought that a boring test
could be so useful? It had
got Ben out of class. Now
it was his turn to escape.
He stuck up his hand.

"Can I go to the toilet
please, miss?"

"You'll have to wait till playtime," Miss Bleet said, looking impatient.

Right, thought Max, *time for Secret Plan: Bursting.* He crossed his legs and bounced up and down on his seat. "Oooh, miss!" he groaned.

But for once Miss Bleet wasn't budging.

Time for Secret Plan: Explosion, Max thought. He held his breath and crossed his eyes.

"He's going to wet himself!" squealed Lucinda.

Max let out a terrible moaning sound. Lucinda shrieked, and Tiffany and Shannon moved their chairs away. Everyone in the class craned their necks to watch.

"OK, you can go," said Miss Bleet hurriedly. "But come straight back."

Max was out of the classroom before she could say homework. He sprinted down the empty corridor, leaped up the

stairs two at a time and burst into the
girls' toilets.

Ben's head peeped out of one of the
cubicles. He beckoned to Max. "I've found
the right window."

Max squeezed in and pushed the door
shut behind him. There was a small open
window above the toilet.

Ben climbed on the seat. "Get up here,"
he said. "It's a great view. But the seat's a
bit dodgy."

Max scrambled up next to him and they
clung to the window ledge, peering out.

"ROOAARR!"

A terrifying, snarling face appeared at the window right in front of them.

"Yow!" cried Max, jumping backwards and knocking into Ben.

CRACK!

The toilet seat broke off its hinges and the two boys tumbled to the floor.

Max sat up. Ben was sitting next to him, the toilet seat round his neck. Max could hear chortling. He looked up at the window to see Toby sticking

his tongue out at them, his golden eyes
shining with mischief.

Suddenly the cubicle door burst open.
Toby ducked out
of sight.

"Max Black
and Ben Neal!"
exclaimed Miss
Bleet. "What
are you doing in
the girls' lavatories?
And *why* are you
wearing a toilet
seat, Ben?"

"I'm not wearing it, miss," began Ben
dizzily. "I was just—"

"I don't want to hear any excuses,"
sighed Miss Bleet. "You can both spend
playtime *and* lunch time tidying the
stock cupboard."

"Boring," grumbled Max as they
trailed back to class. "Bet she won't let us

run beetle races or stick crayons up our noses like we did last time."

"And we won't be able to see Toby again till after school!" added Ben miserably.

For the rest of the day Max and Ben did everything they could to get out of the classroom, but nothing worked – not even when Max told Miss Bleet he'd been bitten by a super-poisonous spider and needed to go to the nurse.

When the bell went, they were first through the door.

"Can you see Toby?" yelled Max as they ran into the playground.

"Not a claw in sight," answered Ben.

Max stopped. A horrible thought had hit him. "Do you think he's gone for good?"

Ben shook his head. "Can't have. He's probably back home on the church."

"Good thinking, Agent Neal," said Max. "Let's search there."

They ran into the churchyard.

"There he is!" shouted Ben, pointing up at the porch. "But he's not moving."

The little monkey-like stone creature was hanging just under the guttering, his mouth in a wide, fixed snarl.

"Hey, Toby," called Max. "Remember us?"

The stone eyes didn't blink. They just stared blankly over the churchyard.

"What's wrong with him?" asked Ben. A look of horror came over his face. "We didn't imagine it, did we?"

"No," Max hissed, pointing. "That's the answer. He's seen Mrs Hogsbum coming."

Their head teacher was steaming down the path towards them.

"What are you doing here?" she demanded. "Have you lost a football on the church roof? School rule number one hundred and thirty-three: boys must not lose footballs on the church roof."

The boys shook their heads.

"**HURUMPH!**" Mrs Hogsbottom glared suspiciously at the guttering.

There was a very rude noise and a **whoosh**, and suddenly a flood of dirty rainwater spewed from Toby's open mouth straight into the head teacher's face.

Max and Ben burst out laughing. Mrs Hogsbum's grey hair was plastered to her head like a swimming cap.

A tangle of leaves and old pine cones
was stuck over one ear and her mascara
had run. She looked like a
demented zebra.

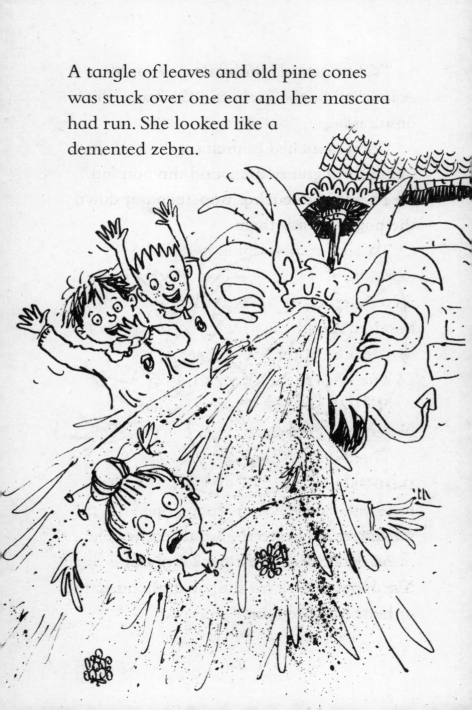

"Outrageous!" she spluttered as she squelched back to school. "Go home this instant!"

Toby launched himself off the gutter and zoomed around the boys' heads, doing victory loop-the-loops.

"Spluttering gutterz!" he yelled as he went. "That's the best trick I've done since I dropped a slug on the vicar's head in the middle of a wedding."

"It was awesome," laughed Max. "And you can really fly! That's awesome too!"

"*Totally* awesome!" agreed Ben, watching Toby swooping up and down in glee.

Toby waved merrily. "Got to go. See you!" And, with that, he flew over the church tower and out of sight.

"I never thought I'd say this," said Ben, "but I'm really looking forward to school tomorrow."

"Me too." Max grinned. "We're going to have the best fun ever now that Toby's our friend!"

WORDSEARCH

Activate your spy radar to find the hidden words - look carefully, they could be up or down, or even backwards!

U	T	M	D	S	Y	F	R	C	T	W	Y
A	G	P	Q	N	L	B	F	R	Z	J	D
T	U	A	Z	U	J	O	O	S	N	A	O
C	H	U	R	C	H	T	O	T	E	V	P
C	L	M	Q	G	C	B	T	O	B	N	N
E	N	O	T	S	O	A	B	W	U	G	O
I	O	F	N	J	E	Y	A	B	L	E	I
C	G	X	O	B	W	L	L	Y	B	P	S
O	L	D	A	C	R	E	L	E	T	C	S
H	A	V	S	M	P	O	W	J	B	V	I
S	T	O	O	B	Y	S	S	O	B	O	M
Z	L	V	K	X	K	A	V	B	G	O	F

Words:

Ben

church

Bossyboots

Toby

mission

Max

stone

Oldacre

football

gargoyle

Kitten Caper

Secret Agent Max Black strolled along the
road on his way to school. He heard the
sound of wheels racing over the pavement
and turned on his spy radar: blond hair,
blue eyes, battered knee pads. It was
Agent Ben Neal, riding a gleaming new
skateboard.

"Awesome!" Max exclaimed as Ben
stopped and flipped the shiny red board
into his hand. "That's the Speed King!"

"It's new," said Ben proudly. "I've
brought it to show everyone this afternoon
when all the Year Four classes get together

to do Hobbies Talk."

They ran through the school gates.

"Greetingz!"

The monkey face of a cheeky gargoyle was hanging down from the school roof.

Max beamed. "Hello there, Toby." Then he spotted something on the roof behind him. Something small and fluffy. "There's a kitten stuck up there!" he gasped, pointing.

"Poor thing," said Ben. "Can you rescue it, Toby?"

To their surprise Toby burst out laughing. "Spluttering gutterz!" he guffawed. "That's not a kitten. That's my gargoyle friend Theophilus. His special power is meant to be turning into a ferocious tiger but it never works. Theo, say hello to Max and Ben."

As they watched, the tabby ball of fluff gave a determined **miaow**. After a lot of wriggling it slowly changed shape until a gargoyle sat in its place. The new gargoyle had a long, tigerish tail and his golden stone was slightly stripy. His face was a bit like a cat's, with bristling whiskers and small, friendly-looking fangs. He stared at Max and Ben.

"Humanz!" he gasped with an anxious swish of his tail. "Help! They mustn't see us."

"It's OK, Theo." Toby laughed. "These two are my friends. They'll keep our secret."

"That's all right then." Theo beamed at Max and Ben. "Sorry if I frightened you when I was a ferocious tiger."

"You weren't exactly ferocious . . ." began Max.

"Wasn't I?" said Theo.

"And you weren't exactly a tiger," Ben told him.

"Wasn't I?" sighed Theo.

"More of a kitten really," explained Max with an apologetic grin.

"Oh dear," said Theo dejectedly. "I was so sure I'd become a tiger this time. The thing is, I'm only four hundred and twelve years old. I haven't had long to practise."

"You were a very good kitten," Max reassured him.

"Keep practising and you'll be the most ferocious tiger in the world," said Toby. "It'll only take another hundred years or so." He caught sight of the Speed King. "What's that?"

"It's my new skateboard," said Ben, holding it up for him to see.

"New board?" came a harsh voice behind them. Toby and Theo froze into statues.

Max's spy radar picked up trouble: shaved head, big fists, sticky-out ears. He knew what that meant.

It was Enemy Agent Barry Price, also known as The Basher, codename: School Bully.

The next minute The Basher had Ben's skateboard in his hands.

"Give it back, Barry!" Ben pleaded. "You can have a look at it this afternoon when our classes get together."

"No one'll want to see this rubbish," scoffed The Basher. "Not when I show them what I've brought." He tapped his school bag with a gloating grin.

"What *have* you brought then?" asked Max.

"It's a secret," Barry said, and, to their horror, jumped on Ben's skateboard. "See you later!"

He streaked off across the playground,
whooping triumphantly and bashing kids
over as he went.

Suddenly Max saw a tall figure emerging from the school door. Grey hair, beaky nose, face like thunder. He knew what that meant. It was Enemy Agent Mrs Hogsbottom, commonly known as Mrs Hogsbum, codename: Stinky Head Teacher. The Basher zoomed past the door and went **smack!** straight into her, knocking her right off her feet.

"Outrageous!" shrieked Mrs Hogsbottom, staggering up again and staring at Barry with her laser vision. "School rule number twenty-seven. The head teacher must not be run over without permission. I shall keep this

monstrosity until home time."

"I never thought I'd say this," gasped Max, "but Mrs Hogsbum's done us a favour. She's taken the Speed King off The Basher for us."

"I'll go and get it back," said Ben eagerly.

The boys rushed over to the furious head teacher, who was brushing gravel off her bony knees. The Basher stood smirking behind her.

"What do you two want?" she snapped as soon as she saw them.

"The skateboard's mine, Mrs Hogsbottom," Ben began to explain. "Could I have it back please?"

"Certainly not!" sniffed the head teacher. "If you hadn't

lent it to Barry Price this wouldn't have
happened."

"I didn't lend it," said Ben. "He snatched
it." He put on his wide-eyed, pleading
look. It always worked on the dinner
ladies, who gave him extra pudding. It
never worked on Mrs Hogsbottom.

"No excuses," she snapped, picking
up the Speed King and tucking it firmly
under her arm.

"But Ben has to show it to everyone in

class later," pleaded Max. "He brought it in
specially for the talk."

"Ben should have thought of that
when he lent it to Barry Price," said Mrs
Hogsbottom crossly. "He can have it back
after school." She turned on her heel and
marched towards the door.

The Basher poked his face into Ben's.

"What a shame!" he sniggered.

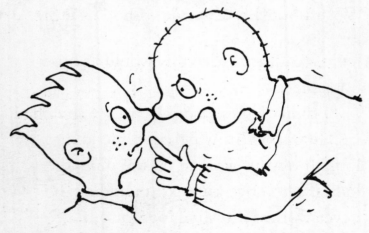

"Still, never mind. No one would have
listened to you whingeing on about
skateboarding. My hobby's much better."

He strutted off, pushing a couple of

small footballers out of the way as he went.

"I don't reckon he's got anything better than your Speed King," said Max when The Basher was out of earshot.

"At least he's got *something*," sighed Ben miserably.

"That was really mean," came a growly purr. Toby was watching The Basher go. "Wish I had my catapult with me. I'd fire some acorns at him."

"When he comes back I'm going to turn into a tiger," said Theo. He stretched out a front paw. Three tiny claws appeared. "That'll give him a scare."

The bell rang. Mrs Hogsbottom stood by the door, fuming.

"We'd better go in," sighed Max, "before she explodes."

"That was the worst morning in the history of worst mornings," said Ben at lunch time. "We haven't played a trick on anyone."

"We've been too busy thinking about how to get our own back on The Basher," Max pointed out.

"And my poor Speed King is being held prisoner," said Ben. "Mrs Hogsbum is probably feeding it to her crocodiles right now."

Max's eyes suddenly lit up. "Don't despair, Agent Neal," he said. "We'll do a great trick and get our own back at the same time." He leaned forward to whisper in Ben's ear, "Barry's got something in his bag that he reckons is really cool, right?"

Ben nodded. "Right, Agent Black."

"Then our mission is to swap it for something stupid and girly." Max grinned. "When he gets it out to show everyone he'll be dead embarrassed."

"Good plan!" breathed Ben. "And I know just the thing – my sister Arabella's ballet tutu. It's all pink and frilly and horrible. It's in her ballet bag. Only one problem," he added with a frown. "The bag is in the girls' cloakroom and boys are not allowed in there. If we get caught we'll never hear the end of it."

"I know someone who can help us with that!" said Max, nodding up at the roof.

"Toby!" exclaimed Ben as their

gargoyle friend waved at them from a gutter. "He could fly in through the cloakroom window and get it for us, no problem."

Making sure no one was looking, the boys sauntered over towards Toby.

"Greetingz!" called Toby chirpily.

"Hi, Toby," Max called back. "Want to help with a trick?"

Toby's yellow eyes lit up and his dragon tail swished. "A trick?" he said eagerly. "A prank? Dangling drainpipes! Tell me all about it!"

Max gave Toby his instructions for Secret Plan: Tutu. Chuckling, the little gargoyle zoomed off to the girls' cloakroom window. In a flash he was back with Arabella's pink tutu in his paws.

"I can hardly bear to touch it, it's so girly," declared Max, pulling a disgusted face. "It's lucky all the school rucksacks look the same. We'll swap my bag for Barry's." He stuffed the tutu in his bag.

"There's one thing we haven't thought of," said Ben. "How are we going to stop The Basher seeing when we swap them round? It's not much of a trick if he catches us at it!"

"Can I join in?" Theo's stripy head popped up over the gutter. "Maybe I'll manage a tiger this time."

"No, we need a kitten," cried Ben, "for Secret Plan: Kitten Diversion. Agent Black, do you remember when that big black cat jumped through the window of our classroom last term? Everyone went all gooey and Miss Bleet forgot to give us any maths homework. Think what would happen if a sweet little tabby kitten came in instead. No one would see us making the bag switch then."

"I like your thinking, Agent Neal," said Max. "Listen, Theo, we've got a trick to play this afternoon and we need everyone to be looking at you while we're setting it up."

A broad grin spread over Theo's whiskery face. "What do I have to do?" he asked, almost falling off the roof in excitement.

"We need you to come in through our classroom window this afternoon," said Max. "While everyone's looking at you, we'll swap The Basher's bag with the one that has the frilly pink tutu in it. All the class will laugh when he gets it out."

"Serve the bully right," said Toby.

"I can do that!" cried Theo.

Just then the bell rang.

"Right!" said Max. "I'll leave a window open for you this afternoon. Come in as soon as we start the lesson. When we've swapped the bags, I'll say the password and you can skedaddle."

"Yes, sir!" Theo sat up proudly. "What's the password?"

"Tiddles," said Max.

Straight after register it was time for Hobbies Talk. The other class in their year group came in, led by Barry.

"Shove up!" he said nastily, pushing a row of girls out of the way.

"Quick," Max whispered to Ben. "Go and grab us a couple of seats behind The Basher. I'll open a window. I hope Theo remembers what to do."

Max joined Ben in the row behind the bully. Barry turned and smirked at the boys.

"I'm looking forward to your talk, Ben," he sneered. "What's it about? Oh yes, I remember. Nothing!"

"Quiet please," came a quavery voice.

Max's spy radar snapped into action:

short and dumpy, limp brown hair, silly half-moon glasses. It was Enemy Agent Miss Bleet, codename: Wimpy Teacher.

"Welcome to Hobbies Talk," Miss Bleet said feebly. "Lucinda, you start."

There was a groan as Lucinda Tellingly marched up to the front clutching her huge collection of plastic ponies.

"I hope Theo comes in soon," muttered Max. "I can't bear to hear much of this."

"These are my special horses," Lucinda began to coo. "They all have names and— Oooh, look at the darling kitten!"

Everyone turned to where she was pointing. Theo, in his cutest tabby form, was perched on the window ledge. He jumped into the room and darted about, as if he was chasing imaginary mice.

"Here, sweetums!" cooed Miss Bleet, bending down. Theo rubbed round her ankles and purred.

"Now's our chance," hissed Max. "All eyes are on Theo, even The Basher's!"

"Ready for synchronized bag switching?" asked Ben.

Max nodded. Ben reached under Barry's chair and snatched up the Basher's bag. Max put his own in its place. Then they both sat back and looked innocent.

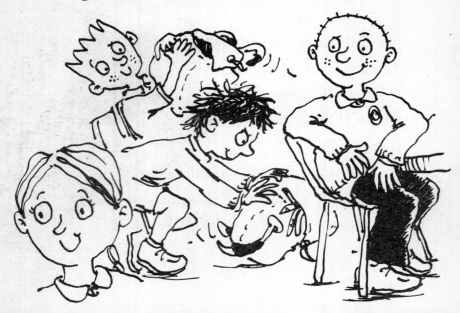

"Tiddles!" Max called. Everyone stared at him in astonishment. "Er . . . I recognize the cat . . . He's called Tiddles and he lives down my road," Max explained with a shrug.

But Theo didn't take his cue and jump out of the window. He was having too much fun. He was now sitting on Miss Bleet's table, playing with her pencil.

"Tiddles!" said Max loudly.

Theo let go of the pencil but rolled over onto his back, looking adorable and knocking Miss Bleet's papers to the floor.

"We won't have time for the trick at this rate," Ben muttered to Max.

"TIDDLES!" yelled Max.

Theo scrambled to his feet and bolted out of the window with a loud **miaow**.

"How mean!" said Lucinda, glaring at Max. "Scaring the poor little thing like that."

"Quiet please," said Miss Bleet, in a fluster. "The cat's gone. Who'd like to go next?"

"But I haven't—" began Lucinda.

"Me!" interrupted Barry Price, grabbing the bag under his chair and marching to the front. "You won't want to listen to anyone else after my go. I've got the best hobby in the world!" He delved into his bag. "Every Saturday I wear this." He pulled out the pink tutu and held it up proudly.

For a long moment there was a shocked silence in the class and then everyone burst out laughing. The Basher suddenly realized what he was holding. He stared at the tutu as if it was a poisonous snake.

"This isn't mine!" he yelled, flinging it to the floor. "Where's my crash helmet? That's what I was going to show you. I do go-karting every weekend."

"You shouldn't be ashamed of enjoying ballet, Barry," said Miss Bleet kindly. "We'd all like to hear about it, wouldn't we, class?"

"YES!" The shout echoed around the
room.

"But I don't do ballet!" Barry made his
way back to his place, his face bright red.

"It's girly. I told you: I do go-karting."

Miss Bleet wasn't listening. "Now tell us all about why you choose to wear a tutu."

"I DON'T WEAR A STUPID TUTU!"

The Basher slumped down in his seat, glaring at everyone. He didn't say another word for the rest of the day. He didn't even notice when Max swapped the bags back.

As soon as the bell rang, Max and Ben dashed off to Mrs Hogsbottom's office to retrieve the Speed King.

"School Rule number four hundred and seventeen," she barked as soon as she saw them. "Boys must not dash into the head teacher's office to get their skateboards back. School rule two hundred and fifty-five . . ."

Five school rules later they were finally released. They ran to the school gate.

"Did you see The Basher's face when he realized what he was holding?" chuckled Ben. "Imagine him go-karting in a tutu!"

"Oh no! Your sister's tutu!" gasped Max. "It's still on the classroom floor!"

Ben turned white. "We're in big trouble. Come on, we've got to get it back without being seen."

They were just heading back towards the school door when something fell on

Ben's head. It was pink and frilly. Max looked up to see Toby on the school roof, with Theo next to him.

"That was a great trick you played on The Basher!" wheezed Toby as Ben struggled with the tutu on his head. "I haven't laughed so much since Theo chased a mouse up the vicar's trousers."

"Thanks, Toby." Max grinned. "And thanks, Theo – you were an awesome kitten."

"You wait till you see my tiger," said Theo. "Only another hundred years and I'll get it perfect."

Ben emerged from under the tutu. "If you go and put this back in Arabella's bag for me," he said, putting his skateboard on the ground, "I'll give you both a ride on my Speed King."

"Spluttering gutterz!" the gargoylz shouted together, grabbing the tutu and rushing off with it.

Fossil Fun

"I can't believe it's time for the school trip at last!" yelled Max as he and Ben roared into the playground in their imaginary super spy plane.

"There's only one thing that could make a day on the beach even better," said Ben.

"Our gargoyle friends coming with us!" Max grinned. "Shame they can't. We'll just have to tell them all about it when we get back." He glanced over the wall at the church next door. "No sign of them," he declared, feeling a little disappointed. "I thought they'd come and see us off."

Just then, Mr Widget blew his whistle.
All the Year Four pupils lined up by
the gate and streamed onto the coach,
laughing and jostling. Max and Ben beat
Lucinda and her friends to the long seat at
the back.

"I saw Theo
and Barney on
the church roof when
we left," Max told Ben as the
coach sped along. "They looked a
bit gloomy."

"Maybe the gargoylz are upset 'cos
they can't come," said Ben.

"Can't come?" said a deep growly voice.

67

A stony face poked out from under the seat in front. It had a wide mouth and the sharpest fangs the boys had ever seen. The strange gargoyle clambered up Max's legs and perched on his knee. He was small and stocky, with the body of a piglet. "Who's going to stop us?"

"Not me!" quavered Max as he and Ben shrank back at the sight of this fierce new gargoyle.

Pop! Zack suddenly appeared out of thin air on the seat between them. Zack's special power was becoming invisible and

the boys never
knew when he
might turn up.

"You boyz
look terrified!" he
guffawed, shaking
his fuzzy mane. "It's
only Cyrus. Say
hello, Cyrus."

The new
gargoyle held out
a paw full of razor-sharp claws. Max and
Ben shook it very carefully.

"Nice to meet you," said Ben politely.

"You'll have to stay out of sight," Max
warned the two gargoylz. "You know you
mustn't be seen by humans – except us,
that is."

"We will!" came a whole chorus of
voices.

Shocked, Max and Ben peered under
their seat. They were greeted by a row

69

of eyes blinking in the dark. Five more
grinning gargoylz shuffled into view.

"Bart . . . Toby . . . Eli . . . Ira . . . Azzan,"
gasped Max, counting along the line.

"Brilliant!" exclaimed Ben. "You're
nearly all here."

"Greetingz!" said Toby, dusting himself
down. "We tried to persuade Theo to come
but he doesn't like water. And Barney said
he'd stay behind to keep him company."

"We've never been to the seaside," said
Bart.

"Speak for yourself, landlubber!" chirped Ira.

The girls in the seat in front turned round and stared.

Max quickly gave them a cheesy grin. "Just doing my pirate impression!" he assured them.

"Shhhh!" Ben warned the stowaway gargoylz. "You don't want to be discovered."

"Max and Ben are the only humanz allowed to see us," Toby solemnly reminded his friends.

"You're lucky to have an old sea dog like me on a trip to the coast," Ira went on in a hoarse whisper. "You'd be lost if a force nine gale or a monster from the deep came along."

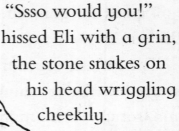

"Ssso would you!"
hissed Eli with a grin,
the stone snakes on
his head wriggling
cheekily.

"You black-
hearted serpent,"
growled Ira. "I've
got the sea in
my blood. You'll
soon be calling me
for help when you're
sucked into a whirlpool."

The gargoylz chattered excitedly all the
way to the beach. Every so often Max or
Ben had to remind them to be quiet.

"Everyone ready?" called Mr Widget
from the front after about half an hour.
"We're nearly there."

"Line up, you motley crew," squawked
Ira. The gargoylz shuffled into an orderly
queue behind him. "We've been watching

72

you all in the playground," Ira explained proudly to the boys.

"You do it very well," whispered Max, impressed. "Better than us!"

"But you can't march out with the rest of us," warned Ben. "You'll be seen. Stay put until everyone's off the coach. We'll see you on the beach."

Max and Ben were the last down the steps of the coach; they joined the rest of Year Four at the top of the cliff path.

"Awesome!" gasped Ben, gazing down at the wide, sunny bay that stretched out invitingly below them.

"Bet there are loads of fossils hidden down there," said Max, pointing at the rocks that lay in a heap against the foot of the cliff. "And we're going to find them all."

Mr Widget climbed back into the coach to check that no one had been left behind.

"Hope the gargoylz have got out!" muttered Ben.

They heard a sharp exclamation and the teacher emerged, his hair standing on end.

"Everything all right, sir?" asked Max. Mr Widget mopped his brow. "I thought I saw a face under the seat – huge mouth, fierce teeth. Terrifying!"

"Probably just a trick of the light," said Ben quickly, trying not to laugh as a line of honey-coloured shapes clambered out of the open coach window

behind Mr Widget and gave the boys a
cheery wave. Luckily the rest of Year Four
were all gazing out at the sea.

Mr Widget shakily led the two classes
down the steep concrete steps to the beach,
where they saw a tall thin man with a
bulging rucksack at his feet waving a
chisel at them.

"Good morning, fossil hunters!" he
called cheerily. "I'm Professor
Bone." He began arranging
interesting lumps of rock
on the sand. "First of all,
who can tell me what
a fossil is?"

Ben put up his
hand eagerly.
"It's a—"

"Prehistoric
creature that's turned
to stone," a rude voice
beside him butted in.

Max turned to look,
his spy radar on full alert:
shaved head, big fists,
nasty grin. He knew
what that meant. It was
Enemy Agent Barry
Price, also known as
The Basher, codename:
School Bully.

SPY FILE:

Codename:
School
Bully

"Exactly!" The professor beamed at
Barry, then held up a rock with a spiral
shape in the middle of it. "I found all these
here on this beach. Do you know what
this one is?" he asked Max.

"Easy," replied Max. "It's—"

"An ammonite," interrupted Barry with
an evil smirk in Max's direction.

"I see we have an expert here," chuckled
Professor Bone. "Ammonites used to swim
in these oceans sixty-five million years
ago." He tipped a pile of sharp, triangular
teeth into his hand. "These are from

prehistoric sharks," he told his wide-eyed audience. "There are plenty of fossils of all sorts around here. Some are loose in the sand and some will be in the rocks. Just keep your eyes open for unusual patterns in the stone and let's see who can find the best ones."

Excited chatter broke out at this.

"That'll be me," shouted Barry over the din. "You lot needn't bother."

He charged off and began to scour the sand. The rest of Year Four followed his lead and scattered across the beach. Soon sand was flying everywhere.

"Basher's such a spoilsport," complained Max as the boys clambered over the rocks they'd seen from the cliff path.

"We'll show him, Agent Black," said Ben, turning over some loose stones. "With our super spying skills we'll sniff out the biggest fossil in the history of biggest fossils. The Basher will be green with envy."

"Maybe the gargoylz will help, Agent Neal," added Max. "Wonder where they are."

"Behind you!" came a ferocious growl. Max and Ben spun round in alarm.

Cyrus and the rest of the gargoylz were watching them from behind a large rock, big grins on their faces.

"You're just in time,"
Max told them, trying to
pretend he hadn't been
scared at all. "We're on
a fossil hunt."

"We'll help! We'll
help!" shouted Zack,
running up and down and
sticking his nose in the sand.
"Er . . . what's a fossil?"

"It's a type of pirate," said Ira
knowledgeably.

"Not exactly," laughed Ben.

As soon as he had told the gargoylz
what to look out for, they were off over the
rocks. All except Ira, who hopped up onto
a boulder. "I'll stay in the crow's nest," he
squawked, shading his eyes with one wing,
"and keep a weather eye out for enemy
attack."

In no time a huge pile of seaweed and
shells had mysteriously appeared on the

sand next to the boys.

Pop! Zack came into view, his paws full of driftwood. "We're champion collectors!" he declared.

"Treasure!" squawked Ira in delight. "Pieces of eight!"

"Er . . . thanks, gargoylz," said Ben, looking doubtfully at the pile of wood as Zack vanished again. He winked at Max. "I don't think we're going to find the best fossil anywhere in this lot."

But Max was scraping at something in the sand. "Look what I've got!" he said, holding up a vicious-looking shark's tooth. "That must have been some fish! This fang's bigger than my hand! There's no way The Basher will do better than that."

"Everyone over here, please!" Mr
Widget called. He was standing on an
upturned bucket and waving
urgently at the diggers.
"Time to hand in
your best fossils."

"Let's show the tooth," said Ben. "The
professor will be knocked out."

But at that moment they heard heavy
footsteps on the sand behind them.

"Man the guns!" shrieked Ira. "We're
under attack!" He hopped behind a rock
just as The Basher pounded up to the pile
of driftwood.

"What a load of rubbish!" he snarled. Then he spotted Max's prize find. His eyes lit up. "I'm having that."

He snatched the shark's tooth right out of Max's hand and sprinted off towards Mr Widget, scattering groups of fossil finders as he went.

"What a cheat!" gasped Ben.

The gargoylz crept out from behind the rocks and Ira reappeared on his lookout perch. They all watched in dismay as Professor Bone praised Barry and displayed the tooth for Year Four to admire.

"That wasn't fair," complained Toby crossly.

"He's a scurvy sea dog!" exclaimed Ira.

"Right, he's not going to spoil our fun any more," said Max. "Let's build a super secret spy base over there, out of sight."

With the help of their gargoyle friends, the boys soon had a fantastic spy headquarters made out of sand. It had a castle tower, a rocket launcher and an underground communications centre covered in shells.

Ira tried to draw a skull and crossbones on the tower with his beak. Suddenly he stopped. "Enemy to starboard! Enemy to starboard!" he squawked, flapping his wings.

Everyone stopped digging.

"It's Barry again," hissed Max urgently, "and he's coming this way. Hide, gargoylz!"

Pop! Zack vanished and the others scuttled out of sight. Max and Ben stood on guard in front of the spy base.

"What a lovely castle!" said Barry, grinning spitefully. Suddenly he gave the boys a hard shove and they toppled backwards – right on top of their creation.

Barry guffawed
and whirled
away like
a tornado
towards his
next victim.

"He's such a
bully," muttered Max,
scrambling out of the
ruins of their spy base.

"Time someone taught him a
lesson," agreed Ben, shaking sand out of
his ear.

Toby scuttled over. "If I had my catapult
I'd get him," he said crossly.

"I could breathe fire and singe his
bottom!" declared Azzan.

"Someone might see you," Ben pointed
out.

"What about me?" said Cyrus, grinning
from ear to ear. "I could use my special
power."

"Is it something really scary?" asked Ben hopefully.

"Not at all," said the fierce little gargoyle. "I sing."

Max frowned. "I don't want to be rude, but how will that help?"

"Cyrus's songs are lullabies," explained Toby.

"And when he sssings one it puts humanz to sssleep. At once," added Eli.

"That's brilliant!" Max grinned. "The Basher can't be a bully if he's *asleep*!"

Barry was now busy throwing Lucinda's shell collection into the sea. Cyrus crept towards him and hid behind a tall sandcastle where no one could see him. Then he flung out his arms, opened his mouth to show all his pointed teeth, and began to sing. Beautiful notes filled the air.

"It's so . . . sweet . . ." Max yawned as the melody washed over him.

"Wish I'd brought my pillow," murmured Ben dreamily.

"Cover your earsss!" hissed Eli urgently. "Or you'll fall asssleep as well."

Max and Ben quickly stuffed their fingers in their ears and watched as Barry gradually slumped to his knees, curled up on the sand and then began to snore. Cyrus finished his lullaby and scuttled back.

The boys took their fingers out of their ears.

"It's gone very quiet," said Ben.

"That's because the singing has worked on everyone!" exclaimed Max. "Look!"

Year Four, their teachers and Professor Bone were all stretched out on the beach, fast asleep.

"Awesome!" said Ben. "We've got the rest of the day to ourselves. What shall we do?"

"Wait a minute." Max turned to Cyrus. "How long will they all stay asleep?"

"Oh, ages!" declared Cyrus fiercely. "Probably all week."

"Ten minutes at most," Toby whispered to Max.

Max looked around at the sleeping figures. "We haven't got long before they wake up then."

"And Barry will be back to his horrible self again," groaned Ben.

"Don't worry, I've got a plan!" said Max. "Let's bury him up to his neck in the sand. When he wakes up, he won't be able to move and we can have fun without him spoiling everything."

"Get digging, landlubbers!" ordered Ira. "All hands to the pump!"

Barry was now lying on his back, sucking his thumb.

As fast as they could, the boys and the gargoylz piled sand all over his body and patted it down hard. Then they covered him in smelly seaweed.

Ira perched on The Basher's chest and glared at him. "Next time it'll be the plank for you, my lad!" he squawked fiercely.

"Good work, everyone," said Ben, stepping back to admire the job. "It'll take Barry ages to get out of that."

"Keep an eye on the landlubbers!" warned Ira.

"They're getting out of their hammocks!"

"I think he means everyone's waking up," explained Ben.

As Year Four and the teachers got to their feet, still yawning, the boys could hear angry shouts from Barry, who was struggling in vain to stand up.

"Leave the dog there a while," advised Ira. "Teach him a lesson."

"Let's play hide-and-seek around the rock pools," said Max. "That'll keep the gargoylz hidden from view. I'll count first."

Ben and the gargoylz shot off to hide.

"Ready or not, here I come," called Max when he got to a hundred.

He leaped over a breakwater and landed on top of Ben. "One down, seven to go!" he declared as Ben joined in the search.

Pop! Zack suddenly appeared in front of them.

"You're supposed to be hiding," exclaimed Max, skidding to a halt.

"Clawz and pincers!" wailed Zack, in a panic. "Clawz and pincers!" The other gargoylz peeped out of their hiding places to see what was going on. Zack suddenly shot off around a rock pool and then vanished again. His stone friends burst out laughing.

"What's going on?" asked Max, puzzled. Then he suddenly leaped in alarm as Zack appeared beside him, hopped up and down and disappeared again. Now Max and Ben could see a very surprised crab being flung about in mid air, attached to the tail of the invisible Zack.

"What do you call a gargoyle with a crab hanging onto his tail?" shrieked Bart, slapping his gladiator skirt in delight.

"I don't know," chorused the others.

"Zack!" spluttered Bart. The gargoylz rolled about on the sand, holding their round bellies and chuckling at the flying crab.

"Stand still, Zack!" called Ben as the crab whipped past his face. "And make yourself visible. Then I can rescue you."

Pop! Zack came into view, shaking his tail with the crab still firmly attached. Ben grabbed hold of the end, gently removed the crab and put it safely in a nearby pool.

"Spluttering gutterz!" gasped Zack. "Ira was right. The seaside's dangerous."

"But it *was* funny," gurgled Toby. "I haven't laughed so much since Cyrus put everyone to sleep in the middle of the vicar's sermon."

"Teacher ahoy!" announced Ira suddenly.

Max looked up. Mr Widget was calling everyone over to the coach.

"Time to go home," sighed Ben.

The gargoylz looked crestfallen.

"You'd better get on board before the rest of us," Max told them.

"Aye, aye." Ira saluted before giving the order. "Form a line, shipmates."

Max and Ben gathered up their things and joined their class.

"Anyone seen Barry Price?" Mr Widget
was asking anxiously.

"Help!" A distant cry echoed across the
sand. "Get me out of here!"

"I think he's stuck, sir," said Ben.

Mr Widget raced over to where Barry
was trapped. The Basher was complaining
loudly.

"How did you manage to bury yourself
in the sand?" they heard the teacher
demanding as he tugged him out.

Max and Ben raced to the back of the coach. They could see a row of eyes under the seat. The engine started and very soon the boys could hear muffled gargoyle snoring.

"That was a great school trip!" said Max as the coach rumbled back towards Oldacre School.

"We've worn the gargoylz out," said Ben with a grin. "No need to keep them quiet this time."

"They didn't even need Cyrus's song to make them fall asleep," Max added with a smile.

"We're not *all* asleep," came a squawk. Ira popped his beak out and winked at the boys. "Someone has to make sure the ship gets safely back to harbour!"

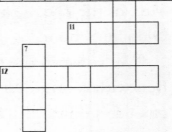

CROSSWORD

Spluttering Gutterz! The vicar loves to do crosswords, and now the gargoylz have made their own!

ACROSS

3. Eli has these coming out of his head (6)
6. These appear when Bart burps! (7)
8. Captain Buckbeak's other name (3)
9. Max and Ben are going _____ at half-term (8)
10. Codename for Barry Price (6, 5)
11. Barry gives the class a laugh when he shows them this (4)
12. The boys make one of these for their science project (7)

DOWN

1. _____ has a very pink party (7)
2. Zack's favourite food (7)
4. _____ uses his long nose to snorkel (3)
5. Rufus can turn into this (8)
7. Ben and Max's first Gargoyle friend (4)

Rocket Ride

Max Black and Ben Neal zoomed up to Oldacre Primary School on their imaginary spy jet-scooters. They wore rucksacks on their backs and were pulling wheelie suitcases behind them. The clock on the church next to the school was just striking six in the morning.

"Here come the world's top superspies on their dawn mission," yelled Max, screeching in at the gates. "All set for a school trip to the Museum of Space and Time in London."

"We're the first ones to arrive, Agent

Black!" exclaimed Ben.

"You know what that means, Agent Neal," said Max with a grin. "Gargoyle time!"

Max and Ben had some unusual friends. They were gargoylz, the little stone statues that hung on the old church. The boys were the only humans who knew the gargoylz could come to life and that each one had a special power. Their favourite thing in the world was playing tricks – which suited Max and Ben perfectly.

Max and Ben whizzed into the churchyard and flung down their cases.

"Strange," said Max. "There's not a gargoyle in sight. I wonder where they are."

All at once there was a loud rumbling snore from the roof of the vicar's house next door. There, curled up in a heap by the chimney, lay Toby, Azzan, Zack and Bart. The boys grinned at each other.

"I'm sure they wouldn't want to be asleep when we're awake, Agent Black," said Ben mischievously.

"Time for a trick, Agent Neal," declared Max.

101

The boys tiptoed up to the vicar's garden wall.

"One . . . two . . . three . . ." whispered Ben.

"GREETINGZ!" the boys yelled.

The pile of gargoylz shot into the air. Zack vanished with a **pop**, Toby flew into a tree and Azzan was so surprised that he let out a blast of flame from his dragony snout, scorching Bart on the bottom. Azzan's special power often got him into trouble.

"It's only us," shouted Max, waving over the wall at them.

Pop! Zack reappeared and the gargoylz beamed at the boys. All except Bart – but he was often grumpy. The chubby little gargoyle flapped at his singed gladiator skirt and grumbled under his breath as he scrambled down to join Max and Ben.

"Dangling drainpipes!" said Toby in his growly purr as he looped the loop over their heads. "That was a good prank, boyz."

"I was very nearly a bonfire!" complained Bart.

"It was only a tiny flame," said Azzan cheerfully.

"It's really early," said Toby, giving a huge yawn.

103

"How come you're at school?"

"Couldn't sleep?" suggested Zack.

Max laughed. "We had to be here early," he told them. "Our class is going on a school trip—"

"—to a museum full of dinosaurs and spaceships!" Ben burst in.

"And the best bit is," added Max in a rush, "we're going to have a sleepover there – tonight!"

"Can we come?" asked Toby, his monkey face full of excitement.

"That's a brilliant idea!" exclaimed Max.

"I like school trips! I like school trips!"

shouted Zack, shaking his mane in delight.

Max and Ben could hear chattering from the playground now. Everyone else was arriving. It was nearly time to go.

"But how can the gargoylz come without being seen?" asked Ben, scratching his head.

"Easy," declared Max. "We can put them in our cases. My mum's packed loads of stuff I don't need – I bet yours has too!"

Ben grinned. "Secret Plan: Pack the Gargoylz."

"We'd better be quick," said Max. He could see his classmates lining up, ready to walk to the station.

The boys grabbed the handles of their wheelie cases and raced off through the playground and into the school.

In two minutes flat they had stuffed their toothbrushes, pyjamas, towels and other useless items under their desks and returned to the churchyard. Max unzipped his case, which now contained a comic, a rolled-up sleeping bag and an odd sock.

Toby immediately jumped in. Azzan bounced in next to him.

"Don't need to hide," insisted Zack. "I'll just disappear."

"It won't work. You know you'll get too excited and end up popping into view," said Ben.

Zack could make himself completely invisible to all humans but he wasn't very good at staying that way.

He ran three times round the church and dived headfirst into Ben's empty case.

"Coming, Bart?" asked Ben.

"Might as well," said the little gargoyle grumpily, "though I don't like museums." He squeezed in beside Zack. "There's not much room," they heard him complain as they zipped up the cases.

Suddenly they heard a booming voice bellowing from the playground. Max's spy radar whirred into action: grey hair, beaky nose, guaranteed to scare the scariest of witches. He knew what that meant. It was Enemy Agent Mrs Hogsbottom, commonly known as Mrs Hogsbum, codename: Evil Head Teacher.

"Outrageous!" she thundered over the wall. "Max Black and Ben Neal, you have broken school rule number five hundred and twenty-two – boys must not loiter in the churchyard when they are going on a school trip to London."

The boys dutifully dragged their cases into the playground and took their places in the line.

"If only Mrs Hogsbum knew who was coming with us!" whispered Max.

"She'd probably explode," replied Ben with a grin.

Their teacher, Miss Bleet, was standing at the front of the line with the other teachers accompanying the class trip, Mr Widget and Mrs Stearn. "Off we go," she called out nervously.

They set off down the road to the railway station.

"Make sure you behave yourselves!" they heard Mrs Hogsbottom yell from the playground. "And don't you dare get lost on the Underground. School rule number one hundred and . . ." Her voice faded as the class went round the corner.

Later that day Max and Ben's class marched up the steps of the Museum of Space and Time and burst through the swing doors.

"Look at that T. rex!" gasped Ben, gawping at the huge skeleton that seemed to fill the whole entrance hall. "It's awesome."

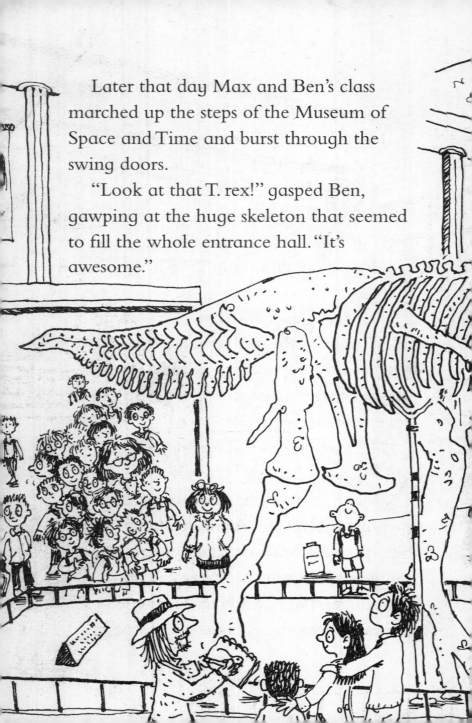

"And the sign over there says **Space Zone**!" gabbled Max excitedly. "This is going to be so cool." A smiling woman with dark hair came over. "Welcome to the museum sleepover experience!" she said brightly.

"I'm Alison – your guide during your stay.
Let's put your cases in our storeroom."

"I want to get out!" came Toby's
growly purr.

Alison looked at Max, puzzled.

"I mean," said Max hurriedly, giving
his case a nudge, "I want to get *into* the
museum."

"You won't have to wait long!" said
their guide. "Follow me."

"We can't leave the gargoylz in our
cases all day," Ben whispered anxiously to
Max. "They'll miss all the fun."

"If we make sure we're last in the storeroom," Max whispered back, "we can let them out when everyone else has gone."

After the rest of the class had run back to the entrance hall, Max and Ben dragged their cases through the storeroom door. The room was small and cramped, stuffed with old furniture and labelled crates. The boys opened their suitcases and Toby, Zack and Azzan burst out. Their faces fell as they stared at the pile of bags.

"Is this it?" asked Zack.

"These aren't very exciting exhibits," said Toby.

Azzan gave a puff of smoke as he sniffed around the cases. "They don't look much like dinosaurs," he complained.

"I told you it wasn't worth coming," said Bart grumpily, poking his head out.

Max and Ben burst out laughing.

"These aren't the exhibits," said Max. "We'll see all the fun stuff in a minute."

"Hop in and you can come with us," said Ben, holding his rucksack open.

Toby dived into Max's bag and Azzan climbed into Ben's.

"Oh dear," said Max. "There's no room for Bart and Zack."

"I'm staying here," said Bart firmly. He zipped himself back into Ben's case, and in a muffled voice added, "I need to catch up on my sleep . . ." Soon loud snores could be heard.

"And I'll just stay invisible," declared

Zack, doing a triple somersault and disappearing with a **pop**.

"Well, make sure you do," warned Max as he opened the door.

Alison was handing out name badges, clipboards and museum maps. "These are for your work," she told the children.

"I hate work!" came Toby's growly voice from Max's rucksack.

"Pardon?" said Alison.

"Er . . ." burbled Max. "I said, 'Great work!'"

"It's nice to see you're so keen," said Alison. "Follow me, everyone."

"I wonder where we're going," said Ben.

"Hope it's the Space section," said Max, eagerly checking his map.

"Or the Earthquake Zone!" added Ben.

"Dinosaurs!" Azzan's muffled voice could be heard from Ben's rucksack.

"Monsters of the deep!" called an invisible Zack from somewhere up a pillar.

But Alison led them into a dull-looking room with display cabinets full of pots that had peculiar bushes growing in them.

"Plants," whispered Max in disgust. "What a waste of time. There are enough of them in my garden at home."

He and Ben stood at the

back of the group while Alison pointed out unusual leaf formations and said long words like "respiration" and "chlorophyll", which the boys didn't understand.

Ben suddenly felt a surge of heat on his back and got a faint whiff of burning plastic. "Can I get out now?" hissed Azzan.

"No," Ben hissed back. "Everyone will see you. And stop melting my rucksack."

Max began to wriggle.

"What's up?" Ben whispered. "You look as if you've got ants in your pants."

"It's Toby," said Max, fidgeting. "He's fed up. He keeps poking me."

At that moment they caught the flash of a dragony tail in the leaves of a banana tree in the corner. It quickly disappeared, but the next instant the whole of Zack could be seen waving cheerily at them from a vine on the ceiling.

"He's forgetting to stay invisible," groaned Ben.

"Emergency, Agent Neal," said Max in a low voice. "We must use our super secret sneaking powers to get the gargoylz away from here before they're discovered."

"And now's our chance, Agent Black!" exclaimed Ben as Alison led the class round a corner towards "Moulds of the World". When everyone was out of sight, the boys ran out into the corridor and dived through the nearest door.

They found themselves in a dimly lit, mysterious-looking room. No one was around. Toby and Azzan scrambled out of the rucksacks.

"About time!" exclaimed Toby. "We've been in there for hourz."

"Dayz probably," said Azzan.

"It's only been ten minutes," Max told them.

Azzan was looking around the room.

"No dinosaurs here either."

Pop! Zack appeared in front of them.
"Who put the lights out?" he asked,
scratching his head.

"It's dark because we're in the Space
Zone," explained Ben, squinting at his
map. "And it's awesome!"

All around the dark room hung
glowing models of the planets,

orbiting a giant sun.
And at the far end was a
gigantic silver rocket. Its pointed
nose almost touched the ceiling.
A TRIP TO THE MOON! said the words over the
rocket door.

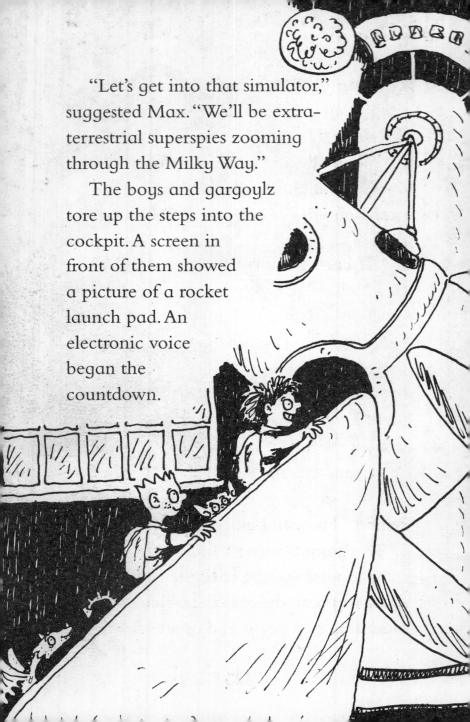

"Let's get into that simulator," suggested Max. "We'll be extra-terrestrial superspies zooming through the Milky Way."

The boys and gargoylz tore up the steps into the cockpit. A screen in front of them showed a picture of a rocket launch pad. An electronic voice began the countdown.

"Ten … nine … eight …"

"Funny way to count," said Azzan.

"Seven … six … five … four …"

"They always count backwards when a rocket's about to take off," said Ben, strapping himself into a seat. "Hold on tight."

"Three … two … one … BLAST OFF!"

There was a deafening roar and the cockpit began to shake violently.

"We're on our way to the moon!" cried Max in excitement.

"It feels like my tummy's on the ceiling!" laughed Ben.

The gargoylz were tumbling around the cockpit, squealing with delight as the ride moved up and down and upside down.

Zack ran up and down the walls and
Azzan blew excited flames and puffs of
smoke into the air.

"Spluttering gutterz!" exclaimed Toby.
"I've never flown like this before."

The simulator jerked and rocked and
spun.

"We're in outer space now!" gasped
Ben, pointing at the stars flashing past on
the screen.

"And we're upside down!" yelled Max as his hair stood on end. "Awesome!"

"**Prepare for touchdown!**" came the electronic voice.

There was a tremendous shaking and a loud thump, and everything was still. The screen showed the moon's surface outside the window. Then the rocket took off and zoomed back to Earth, shaking and tumbling its delighted passengers around again. Finally the cockpit righted itself and the doors to the simulator slid open.

"Fantastic!" exclaimed Max.

"Flame-tastic!" yelled Azzan.

"Shame Bart missed it," said Ben.

Toby grinned. "I haven't had so much fun since Zack jumped on the end of a loose floorboard and catapulted the vicar into the sink."

They clambered dizzily out of the simulator. Toby and Azzan had just scrambled back inside the rucksacks when they heard a voice.

"Max and Ben! What are you doing in here?"

Pop! Zack disappeared. Max's spy radar came to life: small, twitchy, and a nose for smelling trouble at a hundred paces. Max knew what that meant. It was Enemy Agent Mrs Stearn, codename: Strict Supply Teacher. She was standing at the entrance of the Space Zone, glaring at them.

SPY FILE:

Codename: Strict Supply Teacher

"I've been looking for you two," she
snapped. "You should be in the biology
section with everyone else."

"We were doing biology research," said
Ben, trying to stand upright.

Mrs Stearn looked at the rocket
simulator. "What kind of research?" she
demanded.

Max dizzily tried to bring the teacher
into focus. "The effect of space travel on
the human body," he said in a rush. "Did
you know that you get wobbly legs when
you've been to the moon?"

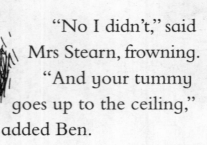

"No I didn't," said
Mrs Stearn, frowning.
"And your tummy
goes up to the ceiling,"
added Ben.

"It's great!" finished Max.
"That doesn't sound like
research to me," sniffed Mrs Stearn.
"You're not to go on the simulator again."

Max and Ben gazed at each other
in disappointment. They'd been looking
forward to having another go.

Just then the rest of the class came in,
gasping with delight at the sight of the
Space Zone. Mrs Stearn went over to
supervise.

"Everyone line up for the space ride,"
called Mr Widget. "Get in line, Max and
Ben."

"Better do what the teacher says!" said
Max, exchanging grins with Ben as they
ran to join the queue.

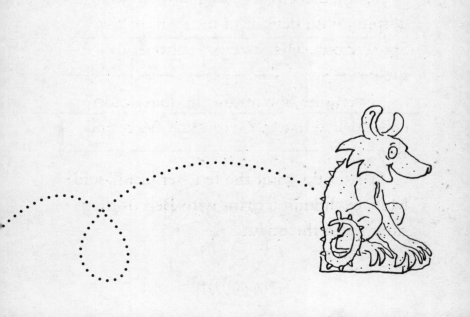

WORD SCRAMBLE

Ben and Max have a message for Toby,
but they've jumbled up the words to stop
Arabella reading it. Can you unscramble
the message?

EW RAE VAHNIG A
LESEP-VROE NI HET
DEGANR TIGHOT. NIRBG
LAL TEH ZORGAGYEL!

__ ___ _____ _

_____-_____ __ ___

_____ _____. _____

___ ___ _____!

Midnight Feast Fun

Max looked at his gargoyle friends, who were sitting in a row on Ben's bed, and grinned. "This is going to be the best sleepover ever!" he declared. "What shall we do first?"

"Cookiez and cake! Cookiez and cake!" shouted Zack, jumping up and down on the duvet.

"They're for later," Max told him. "Ben and I have only just had supper. Anyway, we have to eat them at midnight. That's why it's called a midnight feast."

"Let's play a game," suggested Ben.

"Good thinking, Agent Neal," said Max.
"How about Twister?"

The gargoylz looked puzzled. Max got out a box and laid a big plastic sheet over the floor. On the sheet were different coloured circles.

Toby, Barney and Zack immediately leaped off the bed and jumped in and out of the circles.

Eli turned into a snake and slithered around, tripping them all up.

"Everyone off," laughed Ben. "The game hasn't started yet."

The gargoylz reluctantly stepped off the mat.

"Each time I call out a colour you all put one paw on a circle of that colour," explained Max. He spun an arrow on a card. "And this will tell you which paw. Look, put your front left paw on a red circle and keep it there." He spun again. "Now left back on a green circle. Last one to fall over wins. Eli, you need your paws so you'd better change back."

"Come and join in, Bart," said Ben. "It's a lot of fun."

"Certainly not," grumbled Bart. "Looks much too dangerous to me." And he hid his face in his gladiator skirt.

"Come on, Bart," said Zack, patting him on the back and knocking him off the bed.

"Just one game then," mumbled Bart.

Soon the mat was a tangle of scrambling gargoylz, with Bart in the middle, a big grin on his face.

136

"I'm winning!" Bart declared.

"That's because you're sitting on my wing," moaned Toby.

Suddenly they heard footsteps outside. The gargoylz dived under a chest of drawers just as Ben's mum stuck her head round the door.

"It's getting late, boys," she said, smiling. "No more jumping about. Time to settle down."

She went out again, closing the door. The gargoylz crawled out as Max and Ben quickly pulled on their pyjamas.

"Good game!" exclaimed Zack.

Bart nodded. "Very enjoyable. Especially as I won!"

"No you didn't," laughed Barney. "You pushed us all over!"

"Didn't!" said Bart.

"Did!" said all the other gargoylz.

"Shhhh!" warned Ben. "Mum'll hear."
He pulled out a lilo and began to blow it
up with a foot pump.

"What's that?" asked Theo, poking the
flabby plastic with his paw.

"It's Max's bed," said Ben.

The gargoylz immediately jumped
onto the lilo and rolled about as it
filled with air.

"There's only one thing wrong with this sssleepover," said Eli. "Ben's got his bed and Max has got the ssspare one. Where are *we* going to sssleep?"

"I hadn't thought of that," said Ben. "How about hanging off the windowsill? Or would you feel more at home dangling from the bookshelves?"

"But it's not a proper sssleepover if we don't have a bed like you," said Eli.

Ben ran to the cupboard. "I've got an idea," he grunted as he pulled a sleeping bag and a couple of pillows off the top shelf. "You can sleep in this. It should be big enough for you all."

He opened the sleeping bag up and folded it so that it looked like a bed, with the pillows arranged at the top. The gargoylz piled in excitedly.

"Move up, Zack," said Toby. "And stop those snakes wriggling about, Eli. They tickle. That's it — now we all fit."

Ben put his bedside light on and turned the main one off.

"This is so cosy," purred Theo. "Much better than that bed your sister made."

"Lovely," yawned Barney. "So comfortable . . ." His voice faded out and he fell asleep.

Toby nudged him. "You've got to stay awake for the midnight feast."

Barney jerked awake. "Sorry," he said, with his eyes half closed.

"We've got to do something to keep

him awake," Ben told Max. "It's ages till midnight."

"I've got a plan!" Max winked at him. "Let's tell a spooky story. No one can sleep through that."

"Brilliant, Agent Black," said Ben.

"Don't know any spooky stories," said Toby, looking puzzled. "Do we, gargoylz?" The others shook their heads.

"I know a good one," said Max. "Turn your light off, Ben. We need my multicoloured torch for this."

He sat down next to Ben. Then he shone his torch up under his chin, bathing his face in a ghostly green glow as he began his tale.

"Deep in the dark, dark wood lived a boy," he began in a creepy voice. "And one dark, dark night he went out into the dark, dark wood and—"

He stopped. There were footsteps on the landing outside, getting nearer.

"Dangling drainpipes!" squeaked Barney, his floppy ears pricked up with fright. "It's something scary coming to get us!"

"Worse than that," said Ben. "It's my parents. They must be on their way to bed. Quiet, everybody."

Max turned off his torch and they all sat in the dark, listening as the footsteps went past the door. The footsteps continued

into Ben's parents' bedroom and the door closed. Max switched on the torch again.

"Where was I?" He grinned horribly in the torchlight.

"The dark, dark wood," said Theo in a tiny voice.

"Oh yes. The boy went out into the dark, dark wood and what did he see?"

The gargoylz' eyes grew wider and wider.

"A monster?" whispered Barney.

"A zombie?" quavered Eli, his snakes trembling.

"No," said Max. "He saw something white . . . and floaty . . . and it was coming towards him . . ."

"A ghost!" shrieked the gargoylz in terror.

"It was his friend under a sheet," Max
laughed. "He'd dressed up to scare him!"

He shone his torch around the room.
The gargoylz were lying in a trembling
row, eyes like saucers, clutching the
sleeping bag.

"All awake, I see," said Ben cheerfully.

"Wouldn't dare go to sleep after that
story," whimpered Bart. "It was too scary."

Toby crawled up onto Ben's bed and
gave Max a nudge. "I don't think scary
stories are a good idea," he whispered.
"Not if we want to cheer Bart up."

"You're right," said Max.

"How about telling jokes?" suggested Ben.

"Jokessssss?" Eli looked puzzled. He turned to Theo. "What are jokessss?"

"I don't know," Theo said with a shrug and the other gargoylz shook their heads.

"Jokes are very short, very funny stories," explained Max. "They're meant to make you laugh. Listen – why was the sand wet?"

"We don't know," said Zack. "Why *was* the sand wet?"

Max grinned. "Because the sea weed!"

"Seaweed?" The gargoylz looked at each other in bafflement. Then Toby burst out laughing. "The sea did a wee! That's what made the sand wet!" he explained to his friends. Soon they were all rolling around

146

on the floor holding
their sides. Even Bart
stopped looking
scared and managed
a grin.

"We've got loads
more where that
came from," said Ben.
"What flies through the
air and wobbles?"

"I don't know," chorused the gargoylz,
their eyes shining in the torchlight.

"A jelly-copter!" giggled Ben.

"My turn," said Max. "Why didn't the
skeleton go to the party? Because he had
no*body* to go with!"

The gargoylz shook with laughter
in their little bed. Then they all heard
a strange noise. It was a wheezy, slurpy
sound like water draining down a rusty old
plughole. They looked in amazement to
see Bart holding onto his sides and rocking

backwards and forwards.

"Now I understand jokes," he spluttered. "Listen, I've got one. What do you call a pipe that rain runs along?"

"I don't know," said Ben. "What *do* you call a pipe that rain runs along?"

"A gutter!" chuckled Bart. The other gargoylz fell about laughing.

"That was the best one yet," wheezed Toby, tears of laughter running down his stony cheeks.

"Gutter!" repeated Zack, holding his sides.

Max looked at Ben. "Why is that funny?" he whispered.

"Beats me," said Ben. "I don't think Bart's quite got the hang of jokes yet."

"Well, at least it's cheered him up," Max said happily.

"Gutter!" Bart guffawed loudly, slapping his skirts.

"We'll have to keep the noise down," warned Ben. "My parents might hear – or worse, we might wake up my sister!"

The gargoylz all stopped laughing and looked horrified at the thought.

"Not Arabella!" Theo growled.

Max listened at the door. "It's OK," he said after a moment. "I think everyone's asleep. Time for the midnight feast!"

The gargoylz jumped up and down in excitement as Ben pulled out the bottle of fizzy drink and the chocolate cake.

"Cookiez first! Cookiez first!" chanted Zack, diving under the bed for the box.

Max took off the lid and

his face fell. "I might have known!" he exclaimed bitterly. "Look what my stupid sister's done with the icing."

The others peered into the box. All the cookies were bright girly pink – and decorated with sparkly icing stars and fairies. Some of them had writing on.

Max picked up the biggest cookie. "*Boys smell*," he read.

"Here's another one," said Toby. "*Boys are stupid*."

The gargoylz hooted with laughter.

"What do you call a boy with girly cookiez?" chortled Bart.

"I don't know," said Toby, his eyes bright with mischief.

"MAX!" crowed Bart.

The gargoylz rolled about their bed in delight.

Max took the cookie box and sat on his bed. "Well, if only girls eat pink cookies, then you lot won't be wanting any

and I've got them all to myself," he said
smugly, taking a big bite. "Delicious!" he
sighed.

"We didn't say we didn't want one," said
Barney, horrified. "I'm sure they're lovely."

"Yes." Toby nodded hurriedly. "Pink
cookiez are probably the best. We'd better
taste one to make sure."

Max grinned. "Go on then. Pass the
choccy cake, Ben."

For the next ten minutes the only
sound that could be heard was a happy
chomping and slurping. Bart made them
all giggle when the fizzy drink made him
burp and spiders came tumbling out of his
mouth.

Soon there were only a few cookies left.

"Dangling drainpipes!" said Toby, leaning back, his hands over his fat belly. "That was lovely."

"What do we do next on a sleepover?" asked Theo.

"Well, we could go to sleep, I suppose," said Ben.

"More jokes!" came Bart's gurgly voice.

"OK," said Ben. "Why did the ghost—"

"Quiet!" said Toby. "There are footsteps approaching."

"I can't hear anything," whispered Max, listening hard.

"Gargoylz have sssuper-sssensitive hearing," said Eli. "I can hear them too."

"Hide!" hissed Ben as he dived beneath his covers. Max jumped onto his bed. He heard the gargoylz scuttle under Ben's

bed, dragging the cake tins with them.
He suddenly remembered the drink. He
grabbed the bottle, shoved it under his
duvet and switched off the torch. And just
in time.

The door to the bedroom was flung
open and a figure stood there, outlined by
the landing light. Max's radar burst into
life: fluffy slippers, frilly nightdress, a look
that could kill at ten paces. He knew what
that meant. It was Enemy Agent Arabella
Neal. Codename: Manic Monitor.

"Got you!" shouted Arabella.
"You're mucking around and I'm
telling. You're in big trouble and
you deserve it after taking
away my kitten. MUM!
DAD!"

Footsteps could be
heard running along the
landing. Max knew he
had to do something

quickly. He had an idea. "What's going on?" he groaned as Ben's dad came into the room. Then he sat up and rubbed his eyes. "Why did you wake me up?"

Ben pretended he was still asleep. "I'm having a nightmare!" he wailed. "There's a monster in the doorway. It's got fluffy slippers and it's *sooo* ugly."

"Arabella!" Ben's dad sounded angry. "What are you doing out of bed?"

"The boys were—"

"Is this your idea of a joke?" growled Ben's dad. "The boys were fast asleep and you've woken them up. Go to bed – and I don't want to hear another peep out of you until morning."

Arabella stomped off.

"Sorry, boys," whispered Ben's dad. "Back to sleep now." He closed the door softly.

When it was safe, Max switched on the torch.

"There are still some cookies left," Ben said, peering into the tin. The gargoylz scrambled eagerly out from under the bed and tucked in.

"I haven't had such a tasty feast since I ate the vicar's holly bush," said Toby happily, wiping crumbs from his mouth.

"I've got another joke," declared Bart. "What did the cookie say when his friend was run over by a steamroller?"

"Tell us, Bart," said Max, exchanging a look with Ben. He could tell they were both wondering if it would be a real joke this time or another 'Bart Special'.

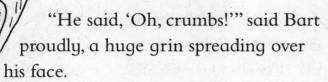

"He said, 'Oh, crumbs!'" said Bart proudly, a huge grin spreading over his face.

Max and Ben did a high-five as their gargoyle friends bounced around and laughed uproariously.

"Success, Agent Black," said Ben. "Not only have we outwitted Arabella and cheered up Bart, but he's got the hang of jokes!"

"Missions accomplished, Agent Neal," agreed Max. "This is officially the best sleepover in the history of sleepovers!"

MAZE

Help Zack and Toby find the delicious cookies Ben's mum has made for the midnight feast!

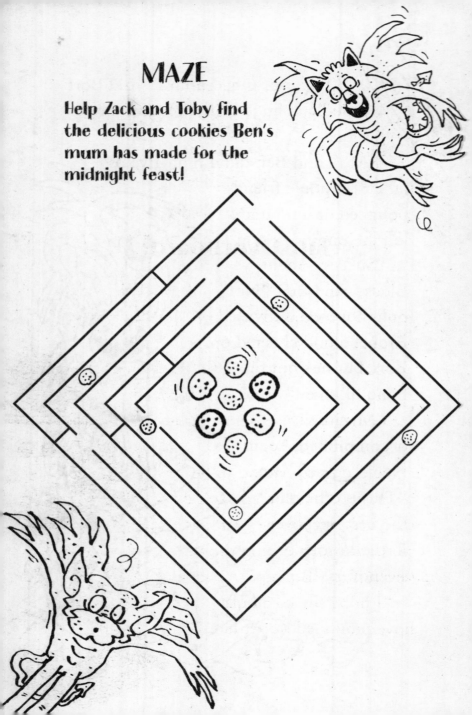

Man Overboard!

It was Saturday afternoon – and Barry's party was about to begin.

Max waved goodbye to his mum as she drove off, then he and Ben zoomed through the turnstile into Pirate Reef Water Park.

"This party's going to be awesome!" exclaimed Max as they sped along the corridor to the boys' changing room, "even if it is Barry's."

"I hope the gargoylz have managed to get here,"

said Ben, looking around eagerly for any sign of their cheeky friends.

"The sooner we're in the water, the sooner we'll find out," declared Max. "That's where I'd be if I was a gargoyle."

"Turn on Secret Agent turbo speed," ordered Ben, flinging open the door of the changing room and pulling off his clothes.

Max quickly unrolled his towel to get his swimming shorts. A very small, very pink, very frilly swimming costume fell out.

"Aaargghhh!" Max cried in horror.

"Disaster, Agent Neal! Mum's packed my little sister Jessica's costume instead of mine."

"We mustn't let Barry know what's happened," said Ben, holding up the frilly pink costume in disgust. "He'll tell the whole party."

"He'll tell everyone in the park," agreed Max glumly.

"Everyone at school," added Ben.

"Everyone in the world . . ."

"Everyone in the universe . . ."

The changing-room door opened. Max and Ben scrambled to cover up the horrible pink costume with their towels.

Max's spy radar burst into life: tall and gangly, black hair, friendly smile. He knew what that meant. It was Duncan Davis, codename: Friendly Classmate. They breathed a sigh of relief.

SPY FILE:

Codename:
Friendly
Classmate

"Cheer up!" said Duncan, looking at Max's gloomy expression. "This is going to be a great party – even if it is Barry's."

"I know," sighed Max, "and I want to get out there, I really do, but I can't." He told Duncan about the dreadful swimsuit mix-up. He knew Duncan wouldn't blab. "I'll just have to watch," he finished miserably.

"I'll say I've had seventeen sausages for lunch and I'll sink if I go in." He slumped down on the bench.

"I'm not swimming if you can't," said Ben loyally.

"It's OK. You can both swim," said Duncan. "I've got a spare pair of swimming shorts. Here you are, Max."

Ben grinned and Max's
eyes lit up. "You're a star,
Duncan!" he exclaimed.
"We won't forget this.
Let's get out there!"

Twenty seconds later Max
and Ben were charging
through the footbath towards
the water. They stopped in amazement at
the sight of the huge pools and slides in
front of them.

"This is the best water park in the
history of best water parks!" declared Ben.

"Look at that flume!" gasped Max, staring goggle-eyed at the long blue tube that twisted its way overhead and down into a swirling splash pool.

"There's a river!" shouted Ben.

"And rapids!" yelled Max.

"There's so much to do!" whooped Ben.

The partygoers were gathering around Barry, who was on an island in the middle of the main pool dressed in bright orange swimming shorts. He was shouting out the rules of his party. There was only one: he must have first go on everything.

"Let's keep well clear of him," suggested Ben.

Max nodded, then he spotted something amazing.

"Thanks to my super detective spy brain, I know where the gargoylz will be – if they've managed to get here," he said. "Look!" He pointed excitedly.

At the far end of the park stood a magnificent full-size pirate ship. It was painted black and gold, with great billowing sails, rows of cannon that squirted water and a skull-and-crossbones flag flapping from its mainmast.

"Wow!" exclaimed Ben. "You're right, Agent Black. That's where the gargoylz will be."

"Let's use our superspy jet packs and get there at top speed," said Max.

"They'll have to be the super-slow ones," Ben pointed out, nodding towards a big sign that said 'no running'.

The boys walked as fast as they dared around the edge of the pool to the pirate ship.

"Great," said Max as they ran up the gangplank. "We're the only people on board. Now, where are those gargoylz?"

He looked over the deck, which was littered with inflatable barrels and pirate chests.

Ben trained his superspy watching devices – codename: eyes – on the ship's wheel. Perched on top of it was Ira, keeping a stern lookout over the water.

"Ahoy there, Ira!" yelled Ben.

The parroty gargoyle gave a squawk
and nearly fell off the wheel.

Max laughed. "It's only us."

"Do that again and I'll make you
scrub the decks, you scurvy seadogz," said
Ira, rearranging his feathers and trying to
look dignified. "I'm in charge of this ship.
Captain Blackbeak's the name."

"Sorry, Captain Blackbeak," said Max.
"We're just so pleased you've come."

"Wouldn't have missed Barry the
Bashbeard's party for all the gold in
Davy Jones's locker," said Ira, cheering up
immediately.

"How did you get here?" asked Ben.
There was a loud **pop!** from the
rigging overhead, and the boys looked
up to see Zack hanging upside
down.

"Hitched a lift!" he called.
"We stowed away in The
Bashbeard's cargo hold,"
Ira told them.

"Hid in his car boot,"
explained Zack with a
grin.

"And here we
are," Ira went on. "All
shipshape and ready
for pirate fun. I was
delighted to find my
fearsome ship all rigged and
ready for me," he added proudly.
"Toby, Barney, Neb and I are his
cutthroat crew," said Zack.
"And this vessel's called the Grinning

Gargoyle," finished Ira.

"But I can only see you and Zack," said Ben, puzzled.

Ira pulled out a telescope and put it to his eye. "I've borrowed the vicar's spyglass," he told the boys. "Over there is shipmate Barney, on the high seaz, keeping a weather eye out for stormz. The rest of the crew are here somewhere ..."

The boys scanned the water park and soon spotted the small, stony figure of Barney, splashing happily about in a rubber ring, hidden from everyone by a model whale.

"Reporting for duty!" came a cheery voice. One of the water cannons seemed to be talking to them. As they looked closely, they could just make out Neb, blending in with the bright gold plastic.

"Good pirate camouflage." Ira nodded approvingly.

"Where's Toby?" asked Max.

"He's walking the plank," declared Captain Blackbeak. "He played a perilous prank on his captain." He pointed fiercely towards a wooden diving board that stuck out from the side of the ship. Toby was wobbling on the end over a deep splash pool.

"Are you OK, Toby?" called Ben. He and Max ran to the ship's rail. "You look a bit scared."

"Greetingz, boyz!" Toby replied. "Don't worry about me. Walking the plank's no problem when you can fly. But I have to pretend I'm frightened for Ira's sake." He looked down at the water below and gave a dramatic shiver. "Don't make me jump, Captain!" he pleaded loudly. "I'm scared of heights. I can't swim. I'll be a good pirate—"

"Enough of your caterwauling!" growled Ira, pointing his telescope at the shaking Toby. "The sharks are waiting to feast on your stony bones."

Toby wiped a paw across his eyes. "Farewell, everyone!" He gave a heavy sigh and winked at Max and Ben. "Here I go!" He tottered to the very end of the plank and then plummeted out of sight.

Max and Ben leaned over the side of the ship.

For a moment they couldn't see anything. Then they spotted Toby swooping merrily round in circles just above the water. He flew back up to join them.

"Good one, Toby!" said Max, impressed. "What perilous prank did you play on Captain Blackbeak?"

Toby chuckled. "I told him there were pieces of eight in that chest over there."

"That's pirate speak for treasure!" gasped Ben.

"He wasn't very pleased when he found out what the treasure really was—" said Toby.

"Three bottle tops and a lump of silver foil," chanted Zack, popping up next to them.

Max and Ben laughed.

"He's a lily-livered gargoyle!" screeched Ira from the wheel. "Treasure is serious business."

"You have to admit it was a good prank though!" said Max.

Ira grinned. "Aye, it was that!" he squawked.

"What shall we do next?" asked Ben. "We haven't explored all of the water park yet." He and Max gazed around at the pools and slides.

"Look at The Basher," cried Max suddenly. "He's out to make trouble."

Barry Price was swimming around the edge of the big pool, an evil grin on his face. He sneaked up behind Duncan, who was floating about on a large lilo, and tipped him overboard! With a roar, The Basher scrambled quickly onto it as Duncan struggled back to the surface.

"That's not fair, Barry," Duncan protested. "Why don't you get one of your own?"

Barry shrugged. "I can't be bothered," he said. "And it's my party. I can do what I like." He paddled away, laughing nastily.

"We can't let Barry get away with that, Agent Black!" exclaimed Ben crossly.

"Too right, Agent Neal," agreed Max. "Duncan helped me out – now it's time to do him a good turn."

"Secret Plan: Get Duncan's Lilo Back," announced Ben.

"We'll help! We'll help!" insisted Zack.

"I give you all special permission to leave the ship and carry out the secret pirate plan," said Ira solemnly. "And mind you don't fail or you'll *all* be walking the plank!"

"Don't worry, Captain Blackbeak," said Max, "superspy pirates like us won't fail."

"I'll man the ship and keep a lookout," said Ira, taking his position on the prow, one wing shading his beady eyes.

Making sure no one was watching, Toby, Zack, Barney, Neb and the boys slid down the escape slide that curved right round the front of the ship and plunged into the water.

"Take up spy positions," hissed Max. Everyone dived behind a coral reef and peered out at Barry.

He was zooming round the pool on the lilo, bashing into anyone who got in his way.

"He's spoiling the party for everybody," said Max.

"Tip him off! Tip him off!" chanted Zack. But before the others could do anything, there was a loud **pop!** and he'd vanished. Soon they could see a line of churning waves and huge splashes making straight for The Basher. A dragony tail was sticking up like a periscope.

"That's no
good," groaned
Ben. "Barry will see
him coming."
Max plunged under
the water and swam
after the little gargoyle.
Soon he was back,
wrestling with a squirming Zack.

"How did you find me?" Zack
demanded. "I was invisible to all humanz."

Max laughed. "Your tail wasn't. Barry
would have known something funny was
going on."

"Whoops!" said Zack with a grin. "I
must have got too excited."

"We need another way to make our
secret plan work," said Ben. "Everyone
have a think."

"What if I tickle his feet?" suggested
Toby. "That'll make him fall off the lilo."

"But he'll spot you doing it," Max

pointed out.

"Not if I get a tickle-stick . . ." Toby swam off and came back holding a long twig from a nearby bush. Then he set off for the lilo, swimming very slowly underwater.

As soon as he was close enough, he wiggled the stick at Barry's feet.

"Gerroff!" snarled Barry, twitching. "Stupid fly." The lilo wobbled dangerously but he clung on. Toby poked the twig out again. This time Barry tried to rub his feet together to get rid of the itch. It was a mistake. The lilo turned over and **splash!** The Basher was in the pool.

The boys laughed.

"Mission accomplished!" declared Toby as he popped up again beside his friends. "Bashbeard defeated!"

"I'm not so sure," said Ben. "Look."

The Basher was scrambling back onto the lilo before anyone else could get to it. His face was like thunder.

"We've got to get him off somehow," said Max determinedly. "I owe it to Duncan."

At that moment Ben noticed Neb, swimming around them underwater, his long nose poking up out of the pool like a snorkel. The little gargoyle surfaced beside them.

"I've got an idea to make our secret plan work," said Ben. "And I know the very gargoyle to do it."

"Is it me again?" asked Zack hopefully.

"No, Zack, it's Neb," said Ben. "He can use his long nose to pull the stopper out of Barry's lilo. All the air will escape and The Basher will sink."

"Brilliant plan, Agent Neal!" exclaimed Max.

"And I'm just the gargoyle for the job!" declared Neb.

He dived under the water and disappeared. His friends watched intently as his small transparent shape whizzed along underwater until it was right beneath Barry's lilo. Then they saw his long nose reach up towards it . . .

Suddenly there was a very rude noise and the lilo shot round and round the pool, air blasting out of its stopper hole. The Basher hung on desperately.

Everyone in the pool stopped to watch. At last the floppy lilo slowly bubbled under the water, taking its astonished

passenger with it. A moment later Barry burst back up to the surface, spluttering.

"Who did that?" he bellowed, peering suspiciously at his guests, who were struggling to hide their laughter. He threw the lilo aside, pulled himself out of the pool and prowled around looking for suspects. An attendant took the lilo off to be blown up again.

"That was perfect!" exclaimed Max as Neb popped up next to him. "You should have seen The Basher's face."

"It's even more perfect," said Ben, pointing. The attendant had brought the inflated lilo back and handed it to the nearest swimmer – who just happened to be Duncan.

The Basher stared angrily at Duncan for a moment. Then he stomped off, muttering something about stupid lilos over his shoulder.

The boys and gargoylz gave a big cheer.

"Mission accomplished!" declared Zack.

"Dangling drainpipes!" chortled Toby.
"I haven't laughed so much since we
had a water fight in the churchyard and
drenched the vicar."

"Uh-oh. The Basher's heading this
way!" Ben hissed suddenly. "And he looks
mad!"

"There's only one thing for it," said
Max. "Everyone to the flume. We'll lie low
till he's gone."

"And have lots of fun while we do,"
said Neb happily.

CODE BREAKER

The Gargoylz have left Ben and Max a message, but to keep it safe from Barry, Toby has used a secret-code. Use the key to crack the code and find where the Gargoylz are!

4 22 22 11   12 10   18 11 11 25 22

— — — —   — —   — — — — —

19 18 20 2   5 23   11 25 22

— — — —   — —   — — —

10 7 6 9 11 10   23 26 22 3 21

— — — — — —   — — — — —

5 22 18 9   11 25 22 25 22 21 24 22.

— — — —   — — — — — — — —

19 18 9 11   25 18 10 18   5 22 14

— — — —   — — — —   — — —

1 6 2 22!

— — — —

Key:

1	2	3	4	5	6	7	8	9	10	11	12	13
J	K	L	M	N	O	P	Q	R	S	T	U	V

14	15	16	17	18	19	20	21	22	23	24	25	26
W	X	Y	Z	A	B	C	D	E	F	G	H	I

Skeleton Scare

"It's Friday evening and it's time for the fair!" exclaimed Max Black, jumping into his imaginary spy rocket and zooming out of Ben's front door. "Let's get there, Agent Neal."

All week Max and his best friend, Ben Neal, had watched the travelling fair being set up on Oldacre village green. Tonight was the opening night!

"Not so fast, Agent Black," said Ben. "We have to wait for my sister and her stupid friend. They're still upstairs doing their hair."

"Arabella and Charlotte should be like

me," said Max. He ran his hands through his spiky brown hair. "See? Ready!"

"If only Mum hadn't said we've all got to go together," moaned Ben. "Yuck! Hope no one sees us walking along with *girls*."

At that moment the boys heard an ear-splitting "*Tee-hee-hee-hee-hee!*" Max's spy radar burst into life. Pink frills, goofy teeth, a laugh that could pierce eardrums.

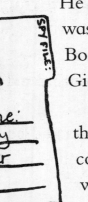

He knew what that meant. It was Enemy Agent Charlotte Boggs, codename: Ghastly Giggler.

"Her giggling's louder than a fire alarm!" complained Ben. "Everyone will look at us."

"Don't worry, Agent Neal," Max whispered as they trailed along the road behind Mrs Neal and the girls. "Super spies like us will soon shake them off at the fair."

At last they arrived at the ticket booth.

"Awesome!"
exclaimed Ben,
gazing at the bright
flashing lights of the
fairground rides.

"Candyfloss!"
sighed Max as the
sweet sugary smell
wafted around them.
"Scrumptious!"

Mrs Neal paid the entrance money and
their hands were stamped with a red big
wheel.

"Now we can go on any ride," said
Ben. "And there's hardly anyone here yet
so there won't be queues."

"We'll start with the carousel," said
Arabella bossily. She pointed a determined
finger at the shiny horses going slowly up
and down.

"*Tee-hee-hee-hee-hee*," giggled Charlotte. "That'll be fun!"

"How boring!" groaned Max.

"And girly!" added Ben.

"Let's find the ghost train!" suggested Max. "I want to go on something spooky."

Ben nodded. "Cool choice!"

"We'll start with the carousel," said Mrs Neal. "After all, Arabella asked first. You can choose next, boys."

Arabella smirked and Charlotte giggled again. Ben looked at Max in horror. They were going to have to stay with the girls for the whole fair – and put up with the Ghastly Giggler!

"Agreed," said Max, to Ben's amazement. "As long as you two don't mind me being sick all over you.

Roundabouts make me ill."

Charlotte stopped mid-giggle.

Arabella's eyes widened with disgust.

"Very well," said Mrs Neal quickly.
"Girls, you go on the carousel and boys,
you can go on the ghost train." Max and
Ben high-fived. "But no mischief," she
warned. "I'll be keeping an eye on you."

"Good thinking, Agent Black,"
commented Ben as he and Max charged
off through the crowds.

"We won't have any more trouble
with them, Agent Neal," answered Max.
"Prepare for a super-scare!"

They zoomed past the dodgems, skirted the hoopla stall and stopped in front of the ghost train.

"Is that it?" said Max in disgust.

Its walls were covered in peeling brown paint and floppy cobwebs. A plastic spider with six legs dangled miserably over the entrance. The sign above said: **THE SCARE OF YOUR LIFE.**

A high-pitched wailing sound was coming from inside.

"How feeble!" exclaimed Max. "It sounds like a mouse with toothache!"

As he spoke, a door at the side opened and a man stepped out wearing a tatty white sheet with two eyeholes.

"If that's a ghost, I'm a pumpkin," said Ben.

"We mustn't give up," said Max. "I expect the fairground people are just making us think it's not scary so we get the fright of our lives when we go in."

Ben cheered up immediately. "You could be right. And it looks old enough to have *real* ghosts in it!" he said. "Let's check it out."

The boys scampered up to the booth, showed their stamped hands and jumped into the front car. The others were empty.

The swing doors flapped open and the car rumbled slowly along a dark tunnel. A weedy scream crackled from a speaker overhead and a ghost on a stick popped up beside them. Round the first corner a coffin lid wobbled open and a vampire with a missing fang sat up and waved. They could see its strings.

"Boring!" scoffed Max.

The car lurched along unsteadily.

Then everything went pitch black and
a deep, hollow laugh echoed through
the dark. A spotlight flashed on, and a
huge, gleaming white skeleton suddenly
appeared in front of them.

"At last!" cried Max, delighted. "Things
are getting spooky!"

But Ben was gripping the safety bar, his
eyes like saucers.

"What's up?" asked Max as the skeleton
walked slowly towards them. "You're not
scared, are you?"

Ben gulped.
"If that's part of
the ride, then how
come it's standing
on the tracks?"

Max froze. Ben was right. The skeleton
was right in front of them — its ghastly
grinning face and long jangling bones lit
eerily by the spotlight. And it wasn't being
worked by strings or sticks! It turned its
empty eye sockets on the boys, staring
long and hard. Then it shook its bony
fingers up and down as if ready to make
a grab for them. The boys yelped in terror.
Next there was a dazzling flash of light
and the skeleton stepped to the side of
the tracks.

"It's alive!" croaked Ben.

"Hello, Max and Ben," the skeleton said in a deep, echoing voice.

Max and Ben leaned as far away from the skeleton as possible while the car chugged slowly past. But they didn't dare take their eyes off it until they had gone round a corner and out of sight.

"Did you see that?" whispered Max.

"It – it knew our names!" stuttered Ben. "It might come after us!"

Suddenly something dropped heavily onto Max's shoulder.

"*Aargghhhh!*" he shrieked, and tried to leap out of the car. "It's got me!"

"Help!" wailed Ben. "We're being attacked!"

"Greetingz!" came a growly purr.

The boys looked up to see Toby, their gargoyle friend, his eyes shining with mischief!

He hopped down onto Max's lap. "How did you get here?" gasped Ben.

"You gave us such a fright!" said Max.

"We saw the fair being set up from the church spire," said Toby, flapping his wings and screwing up his monkey face excitedly. "It looked like fun so most of the gargoylz have come along."

The gargoylz were little carved stone creatures who lived on the church next door to the boys' school. Max and Ben were the only humans who knew that they were alive and that they all had special powers – which were great for playing tricks on people.

"We didn't want to miss the fun," called

an eager voice, and Azzan jumped into the front of the car. Theo landed beside him, waving his stripy tail in delight.

"I wouldn't stay here," Max warned them. He glanced around nervously. "There's a really spooky skeleton somewhere . . ."

The gargoylz burst out laughing.

Azzan chuckled so much he snorted fire from his dragony nose.

"That's Rufus," explained Toby. "He's our friend."

"Your friend?" echoed Max, horrified.

"We heard you say the ghost train

wasn't scary enough so we asked him to help out," said Theo. He gave a happy *miaow*. "And it worked!"

"Y-y-you've got a friend who's a skeleton?" gasped Ben.

"He's a gargoyle ..." began Theo.

"... whose special power is *turning into a skeleton*," finished Azzan.

The boys grinned with relief.

"Cool power!" exclaimed Max. "It must be great for playing tricks."

"He was really scary!" added Ben. "I can't wait to meet him!"

"He'll want to say hello to you too," said Toby.

"We told him you're our friendz," said Azzan, "so it's OK for you to talk to him ..."

"... even though you're humanz," added Theo.

The train passed
a floppy witch
puppet with broken
strings and rattled
on towards some
double doors. The
boys could see
daylight beyond.
The ride was
nearly over.

The gargoylz
jumped out and scampered off.

"Meet us round the back," Toby called
over his shoulder.

When the train ground to a halt,
Max and Ben jumped out and ran round
behind the ride. Toby, Azzan and Theo
were waiting for them.

"Introducing Rufus!" announced Theo.

Something moved the rotten planks at
the back of the ride, and a very strange
gargoyle scrambled out.

Rufus was taller than the other gargoylz, with a huge warty nose and big bulging cheeks. He had wide, hunched shoulders and his muscly arms dangled down to the ground.

"Er, hello," said Ben and Max nervously.

Rufus's face split into an enormous friendly grin. "Hello!" he boomed, waving a pudgy hand. "Did you like my trick?"

"It was awesome," said Max.

"It's not easy," Rufus told them. "But it's very useful for scaring off pesky humanz. Not you two, of course!" he added, giving Max a friendly punch on the arm that nearly knocked him over.

"Show them how you change into a skeleton," said Theo. "Of course, it's not as terrifying as when I turn into a ferocious tiger," he added, "but it's still amazing."

Theo *thought* he became a fierce tiger when he used his special power to change shape, but as he was a very young gargoyle – only 412 years old – he only ever managed a sweet tabby kitten.

"Stand back for a *spook*tacular performance," said Rufus, flexing his massive muscles. He sucked himself in like a balloon deflating. Then, before their amazed eyes, he grew tall and thin and his stone melted away. Now a giant grinning skeleton loomed over the boys, rattling its bones and gnashing its teeth.

Max and Ben clapped wildly as Rufus shrank back into a

gargoyle again and took a bow.

"Got to be off now," Toby said, rubbing his paws together. "We've got lots of rides to try."

The gargoylz scampered away excitedly.

"That sounds like a good idea!" exclaimed Max. "Let's go and try a few more rides too, Agent Neal."

They shot off towards the dodgems and ran straight into Arabella and Charlotte.

"Hello," said Arabella with a beaming smile. She was holding something behind her back.

"Glad we've found you. *Tee-hee-hee-hee-hee!*" Charlotte's giggle was even louder than usual.

"They're up to something," hissed Ben suspiciously.

"Who was scared of a silly little ghost train then?" said Arabella sweetly.

"Poor babies!" snorted Charlotte.

The boys' jaws dropped in amazement.

"How did they know?" Max muttered in Ben's ear.

Arabella pulled a piece of shiny paper out from behind her back and dangled it in front of them. Max and Ben gawped at it. It was a picture of the two boys in the ghost train – their mouths open in utter terror.

"That's us," gasped Ben.

"That flash of light must have been a ride photo," croaked Max. He leaped forward to snatch the embarrassing picture.

But Ben's sister was too quick for him. She whipped it away and skipped off into

the busy face-painting tent.
Charlotte poked her tongue
out and followed, giggling
all the way.

"We can't get it back
from her in there," moaned Ben.
"Someone might see it."

"It's so unfair, Agent Neal," said Max as
they mooched away. "The photo doesn't
show Rufus's super-spooky skeleton.
Anyone would have been scared of that."

"That's true," said Ben, scowling. "But
girls don't care about things like that.
They're totally unreasonable! What we
need, Agent Black, is Secret Plan: Get
Our Own Back."

"That's going to take some thinking,"
said Max. He pointed at the spinning
teacups ride. "And there's the place to do
it. Spinning always helps my brain work."

The boys raced over and clambered
into a teacup. As the ride picked up speed

and the cups began to spin, the boys heard
growly laughter above the music. A spotty
cup flashed by and they caught a glimpse
of three merry stone-coloured creatures
rolling around inside.

"More gargoylz!" shouted Ben in
delight. "There's Zack and Cyrus . . . and
Eli too! I can see the snakes on his head –
they're all tangled together."

"Seeing Cyrus has given me an idea for our secret plan," said Max mysteriously.

As soon as the ride finished, the boys followed their three stony friends to the back of the shooting range.

"We need your help to play a trick on Ben's sister and her awful friend," said Max.

"Yippee!" shouted the gargoylz. "We love tricks."

Max told them about the photo. "So you see how mean the girls are," he explained.

"We want to get our own back on them," added Ben.

Cyrus flexed his long, sharp claws and put on his fiercest face. "I'll frighten them," he growled menacingly.

"Scare the girlz! Scare the girlz!" chanted Zack, shaking his mane excitedly, while Eli's snakes wriggled in delight.

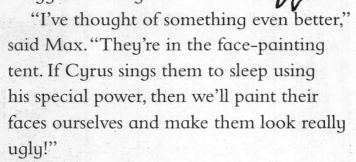

"I've thought of something even better," said Max. "They're in the face-painting tent. If Cyrus sings them to sleep using his special power, then we'll paint their faces ourselves and make them look really ugly!"

"Well," added Ben, "more ugly than *usual*, anyway."

"Cyrus, you turn to stone and I'll carry you in there," said Max. "Everyone will think you're a prize I won from a stall."

"We'll help with the painting," said Eli. "I'll turn into a grasss snake and ssslither in. Then I won't be seen."

"I'll vanish from sight!" yelled Zack, disappearing with an excited **pop!**

Cyrus froze into stone. Max picked him up and marched into the tent. Ben followed behind.

Arabella and Charlotte were having beautiful butterfly wings painted on their cheeks.

"What have you got there?" demanded Arabella, glaring at Cyrus. "It's very ugly."

"*Tee-hee-hee-hee-hee!*" Charlotte tittered.

Max felt Cyrus twitch crossly. "I won it," he said, dumping the frowning gargoyle on Arabella's lap. "If you press its tummy, it sings."

Arabella prodded Cyrus hard.

Ben and Max quickly put their fingers in their ears. They knew Cyrus's power worked on anybody who heard him sing.

Cyrus flung out his arms, opened his mouth and sang a beautiful lullaby at the top of his voice. Snores soon echoed round the tent as, one by one, everyone fell asleep. Zack appeared with a **pop!** and Eli turned from grass snake to gargoyle. Then they all dived headfirst into the box of face paints.

"We'd better hurry before they wake up," said Max.

"Take your time," growled Cyrus. "My song's so powerful they'll stay asleep all night."

"He'sss just boasting as usual," Eli reminded them. "It'll be ten minutesss at the mossst."

Ben put black circles round his sister's eyes and painted a big jagged scar across her cheek.

Max covered Charlotte's face in green paint. Then he drew long white fangs down from her mouth.

The gargoylz blobbed coloured splodges all over the girls' noses.

"Spluttering gutterz!" said Cyrus. "We've done a good job."

"They look like something out of a horror movie," agreed Ben in delight. "Now it's their turn to be embarrassed. I wish we had a camera."

"Gruesome girlz! Gruesome girlz!" declared Zack enthusiastically.

The snakes on Eli's head hissed with laughter.

"Let's see if we can find that photo of us on the ghost train before they wake up," suggested Max.

Ben started to search Arabella's pockets. "There's no sign of it . . ." he said.

Arabella yawned and stretched.

"They're waking up," warned Max. "Hide!"

Max, Ben and the gargoylz ducked down behind a chair.

Arabella opened her eyes and looked around sleepily. Then she caught sight of herself in the mirror. "*Aaaarggghhhh!*" she screamed.

Charlotte woke with a start and stared at her friend in horror. "Your face!" she squawked.

Arabella gawped at her. "And yours!"

They both looked in the mirror together.

"*Aaaarggggghhhhhh!*" they screeched.

Max and Ben and the gargoylz crawled out under the tent wall and collapsed in a heap, rocking with laughter.

"Thanks, gargoylz," said Ben. "We couldn't have done it without you."

"I haven't had so much fun since Zack painted spotsss on the vicar and he thought he had the measlez!" chuckled Eli.

"More ridez! More ridez!" shouted Zack, and the three gargoylz charged off together.

"Well, we may not have found the photo," said Max, "but we've definitely got our own back on the girls. They look hideous!"

"Yup," Ben agreed, grinning happily. "Those girls are so scary the ghost train could do with them!"

Pink Princess Peril!

"Wheeeeeeeee!"

Max sat bolt upright in his bed wondering what the ear-splitting noise was. He'd been having a lovely dream. Toby had taught him to fly and he'd been dive-bombing Mrs Hogsbum.

"Wasss going on?" demanded a sleepy voice.

Max leaned over the edge of his bed. He could just see Ben's tangled blond hair peeping out from his sleeping bag. "It's coming from downstairs," he told him.

"Sounds like a piglet that's sat on a

pin," grumbled Ben.

"Let's investigate, Agent Neal," suggested Max.

They followed the dreadful screeching down to the lounge.

Jessica was sitting in the middle of the carpet surrounded by pink, shiny wrapping paper. "I'm five!" she squealed. "Look at all my presents!"

Max and Ben
tried to shield their
eyes from the
singing dolls,
fluffy woodland
creatures
and sparkly
hairbands strewn
around the floor.

Max's mum
came in from the
kitchen. "You could
have waited for us, Jess,"
she said. Then she saw the
boys pretending to be sick in the
corner. "That's enough, you two!"

Jessica stuck her tongue out at them
behind her mother's back.

"Haven't you got something to say to
Jessica, Max?" said Mrs Black.

"Happy birthday," muttered Max.

"And your present?" hissed his mother.

"Oh, that!" Max plodded upstairs and pulled out the pink-wrapped parcel from under his bed. His mum had made it look all girly, with ribbons and glitter, but it had got nicely squashed when the boys had played Spy Trampoline on the bed last night. Max blew off the dust, ran back downstairs and thrust it at his sister.

"Here you are," he mumbled. "It was the best one in the shop."

Jessica tore it open. It was a jigsaw with a T. rex eating a Triceratops on it.

"Cool!" said Ben admiringly.

"Yuck!" declared Jessica, throwing it on the floor.

"What do you say, Jessica?" prompted her mother.

"Thanks," grunted Jessica.

Ben held out his present. Jessica took it and unwrapped it. "A pink pony!" she shrieked in delight. "So pretty! Wait till I show my friends."

"My mum chose it, not me," Ben told her, backing away in horror and stepping on her new Terence the Talking Turtle, which began to recite a poem about pixies.

All morning Max and Ben tried to keep out of the way of the party preparations. It wasn't easy: the kitchen was crammed with party plates and napkins, the lounge was stuffed with Jessica's new toys, and Mum was sticking pink streamers and balloons up all over the place.

"The only safe room is the toilet!" Max complained to Ben after lunch. "I'm getting allergic to pink. We need to escape from all this girly birthday stuff."

"Good idea, Agent Black," said Ben. "Time for Secret Plan: Prepare Rucksacks. Your dad's put up the tent. Let's go and hide away in our spy camp at the bottom of the garden."

"Last one there is a sausage!" yelled Max.

Ten minutes later, their rucksacks stuffed with essential equipment, the boys bounded into the garden and nearly crashed into Mr Black. He was fiddling with a huge round bundle wrapped in a tarpaulin.

"The bouncy castle's arrived," he told them.

"We'll help put it up!" offered Max. "Then we can test it out before the princesses come."

Dad switched on the motor. "Soon have it blown up," he said cheerily. He pulled away the covering and the castle slowly filled with air and took shape in front of them.

"Oh, no!" gasped Max.

"It's PINK!"

"*Very* pink," agreed Ben
weakly as a pink turret popped up
into the air, with a jaunty pink flag at
the top.

"*Totally* pink!" croaked Max.

The castle stood majestically on its base. It had four towers entwined with pretty painted roses, and glowed bright pink in the sun.

The boys shuddered.

"Hideous!" declared Ben. "It's more of a pink palace than a bouncy castle. If we go on that, the colour will blind us."

"Too right," agreed Max. "Escape to the spy camp!"

They sprinted for the tent, which Max's dad had set up among the trees at the bottom of the garden. It had been Max's granddad's when he was a boy, and it was big, brown and sturdy.

"I've got all the comics and games," said Ben, pulling out his latest electronic game.

"And I've got the joke books and the action figures," said Max, spilling his bursting bag onto the groundsheet.

Ben and Max had just finished level seven of Attack of the Killer Courgettes when horrible screeches filled the air.

Max peeped out of the tent. His spy radar was fizzing: shriekingly loud, extremely annoying, sparkly crown bobbing up above the pink inflatable turrets. He knew

what that meant. It was
Enemy Agent Jessica
Black, codename:
Disgusting Little
Sister. And she was
surrounded by her
annoying friends on
the bouncy castle.

"Enemy agents on
the loose," said Ben. "They're swarming all
over the pink palace."

"Let's set up a Superspy Warning
System," suggested Max. "Then we'll
know if they come near."

"Good thinking," said Ben.

"If we tie a row of tin cans across the
garden," said Max, "anyone who comes
down here will run into it and make a
terrible clatter."

He fetched an armful of tins from the
recycling and some string. "Now we just
need the washing line." He pulled out a

pair of scissors and was soon back with a trailing length of red plastic cord, pegs still attached.

They tied each can to a piece of string and pegged the cans-on-strings to the washing line in a long jangly row. Then they each took one end of the line and stretched it across the garden.

"I'll fix this end to the trellis," said Ben.

"And I'll tie this end to a tree," said Max.

They stood back to admire their Superspy Warning System as it stretched across the end of the garden at knee height, hidden by the long grass.

"Anyone approaching will definitely set off the alarm, Agent Black," said Ben proudly.

"And the minute we hear it, Agent Neal," said Max with a wink, "we let fly our secret weapon."

He dragged a bucket full of water and several big gloopy sponges out from behind the tent. "Mum and Dad left this here after they washed the garden chairs," he said. "I thought it might come in useful."

"Awesome!" exclaimed Ben. "I hope some nosy girls come along! They'll run straight into our water ambush."

Back inside the tent, Max opened the joke book. "Now for some more fun."

He turned the pages. "Here's a good one. What do you call a dinosaur with only one eye?"

"I don't know," said Ben. "What do you call a dinosaur with only one eye?"

"A Do-you-think-he-saurus!" The boys roared with laughter.

134

Jangle, jingle, jangle!

Ben stopped laughing. "That's the alarm."

"Someone's coming," said Max.

He unzipped the tent opening a little and they peered out.

Max's jaw dropped. A pointy red hat with a pink veil fluttering from the top was bobbing along through the long grass. The tin cans clanged wildly.

"Is it one of the girls?" whispered Ben. "She's very short."

They crept out of the tent and grabbed a wet sponge each.

"Ready . . . aim . . . fire!" yelled Max.

The boys launched their dripping missiles, which hit the hat with a splat.

"Bull's-eye!" cried Ben.

"Spluttering gutterz!" shouted their victim as he came into view.

Max's spy radar jumped into action: monkey face, big pointy ears, flapping

wings. He knew what that meant. It was
Toby. But their little friend was
in disguise! The princess hat
was tied under his chin
with a bit of tinsel and
he wore a sparkly belt
round his tummy.

"Sponges down,"
ordered Max quickly.

"Sorry, Toby," said
Ben, rushing over and
drying him off with his
T-shirt. "We thought you were
a gruesome girl."

"I'm a princess," said Toby indignantly.
"Can't you see? This is the hat your nan
plonked on my head when she thought I
was a garden gnome. I just made it pinker
and prettier."

"But why do you want to be a
princess?" asked Max, horrified. "We're
overrun with princesses as it is."

"It's a princess party, isn't it?" explained
Toby. He gave a loud whistle. The
long grass rippled and the cans
clattered together, making
a terrible din, as six more
gargoylz appeared.

"We're *all* princesses!"
growled Cyrus proudly.

Max and Ben gawped
at them. Cyrus had a
sparkly tiara perched
between his pointy ears.

Rufus wore a satin bridesmaid's
dress stretched over his large frame,
and Barney was shuffling along in pink
fluffy slippers. Zack was dashing about
wrapped in a pink lace curtain. It was
too long, and each time he tripped, he
accidentally vanished with a **pop!**

"Look at Bart!" gasped Ben.

The grumpy little gargoyle wore a
shiny petticoat over his gladiator skirt.

"At least I don't look like a toilet brush," he said sulkily, pointing at Theo.

"I don't look like a toilet brush. I look lovely," insisted Theo. He had a pink ballet tutu around his stripy middle and a bow tied to one ear.

Shrieking with laughter, Max and Ben rolled about on the grass.

"I don't see what's so funny!" huffed
Toby.

The gargoylz were standing in a
line, paws on hips, faces frowning out
from their pink costumes. Max and Ben
laughed even harder.

"We got the costumes ourselves," said
Barney, sounding a little hurt. "From the
church charity box."

"It's a very clever idea!" said Max
quickly.

"And you all look wonderful," added
Ben.

The gargoylz beamed happily.

Pop! Zack disappeared, although his pink lace curtain could still be seen zooming towards the tent. "Where are the cookiez and cakes?" he asked.

"Good point," said Rufus. "It's a party, and partiez are meant to have yummy food."

"There's lots of party food," explained Max, "but—"

"Can we have some then?" Theo interrupted.

"There's a problem," Max went on. "The feast is inside, and the only way to get to it is past the pink palace" – his voice dropped to a horrified whisper – "and that's full of girls."

"I'll go! I'll go!" declared Zack, popping into view. "They won't see me."

"But will you be able to stay invisible when you're faced with pizza and chocolate cake and iced biscuits?" asked Ben. "You know humans mustn't see you."

"Of course!" said Zack.

"No you won't!" chorused the others.

"You always get too excited," grumbled Bart.

"And anyway, your costume will still show," Cyrus added.

"Well, how are we going to get to the food then?" asked Toby.

Max and Ben looked at each other. "We'll have to take on this dangerous mission ourselves, Agent Neal," said Max.

"You'll need a disguise," said Barney,
taking off his fluffy pink slippers. "Put
these on, Max. Lend him your curtain,
Zack."

"I'm not wearing those!" said Max in
alarm.

"You have no choice," said Bart sternly.

"He's right," sighed Ben. "Pass me your
dress, Rufus."

He put on the dress and, swiping the
veil from Toby's hat, draped it over
his face. "Princess Ben at your
service," he trilled, giving a
wobbly curtsy.

The gargoylz burst out
laughing.

Max plonked Toby's
hat on and tied the lacy
curtain round his waist.
"This is a serious mission,"
he told the giggling
gargoylz. "Ben and I are going

deep into enemy territory. We may not make it back without being shrieked at – or, worse, laughed at – by a whole load of five-year-old girls."

"Which way shall we go?" asked Ben.

"Over the rockery, behind the runner beans and under the bird table," said Max. "Then we'll take cover behind the dustbins before the final dash. After that it's down the side path to the front door. No one will be expecting that. We can join the line of princesses waiting to come in. Jessica's invited thousands so there's sure to be some still arriving."

Max and Ben set off. They stepped
carefully over their tin-can alarm system
and skipped across to the rockery like little
princesses. Soon they were peering round
the corner of the
house into the
front garden.

A line of
excited five-year-
olds in princess
costumes stretched
away from the
front door.

"Good," said Max. "It's Dad at the
door. He won't notice it's us."

"Let's go!" hissed Ben.

They trotted out from their hiding
place and joined the back of the queue. As
they went past Dad, they kept their heads
down.

"Nice frock," said Mr Black as Ben
slunk past.

The boys zoomed into the lounge.
Every centimetre of the room
was covered in sparkly
pink decorations.

"It's so girly!"
gasped Ben. "It's
enough to make
a superspy
collapse with
pink poisoning."

"We have to
brave it," said
Max grimly,
"or starve."

Pushing aside
the pink streamers
and balloons, they
made for the table.
Fantastic food filled
every space.

"Look at this feast!"
said Max. "Doughnuts,

cookies, crisps, sausage rolls.
I don't know where to
start."

Ben grabbed some
chocolate fingers
and cheese sticks.
"How are we going
to carry this?" he
asked suddenly.
"We haven't got
any pockets."

Max held the
lace curtain out
in front of him.
"This makes a
great food sling,"
he said. Ben did
the same with the
bridesmaid's dress.
They filled their
skirts with goodies at
mega spy-speed.

"Let's get back to the gargoylz," said Max, waddling towards the door. "We'll take the kitchen route."

They crept into the hall. It was empty. So far, so good.

But they had just got to the kitchen door when a horrible shrill squeal filled the air.

"Aaaaaaaaaaah!"

The boys spun round. Jessica was standing by the stairs.

"Max and Ben are princesses!" she mocked. "Max and Ben are princesses!"

All at once the hall was full of screaming girls, laughing at them.

Max thought he would explode with the horror of it all. He and Ben had to escape — and quickly. He thought hard. "Oooh!" he cried in a silly voice. "What a lovely fluffy-wuffy little kitten! It just ran upstairs."

At once the girls gave chase in a squealing swarm.

"RUN, BEN!" yelled Max.

The boys didn't stop until they'd reached the tent.

"That fooled them," said Ben. "And we didn't lose a single iced bun."

The tent flap opened and Bart peered out. "Hurry up out there," he said grumpily. "We're hungry."

The boys spilled the feast onto the tent floor. The cakes were a bit squashed and mixed up with the crisps, but the gargoylz fell on them.

"Mmm!" said Ben, munching a sausage roll covered in sprinkles. "This is a great combination."

"It's the best feast I've had since we nibbled all the vicar's scones and he thought he had mice," said Toby.

"I like princess parties," said Barney happily.

"If a princess party means a fantastic feast in a tent with your friends, then so do I!" declared Max.

Holiday Plans

Max Black screeched up to his best friend's house on his imaginary spy turbo-rocket – codename: bicycle.

Awesome, he thought. *It's half-term. There's no school for a week and I'm going to spend the whole day with Ben.*

Ben Neal flung open the door. He had a huge grin on his face. "Ready to make holiday plans with the gargoylz, Agent Black?" he said.

"Ready, Agent Neal!" replied Max eagerly. "Get your bike and we'll go and see them."

The gargoylz were Max and Ben's top-secret friends. Everyone else in Oldacre thought they were just ugly stone statues carved all over the church next to the boys' school. Only Max and Ben knew that the mischievous little creatures were alive – and ready to play all sorts of tricks, using their special powers.

A dreadful screeching noise suddenly filled the house. "Has someone trodden on a cat?" Max asked.

"It's worse than that," said Ben, covering his ears. "Arabella's singing!"

"That's given me a cool idea," said Max, his eyes wide with mischief. "Before we see the gargoylz, let's practise our secret agent skills by spying on your sister."

Ben gave him a high-five. "Brilliant plan!" he exclaimed.

Grabbing their superspy info-collecting kit – codename: notebooks and pencils – they crept along the hall towards the ghastly sound.

"It's coming from the dining room," hissed Max. "She mustn't see us."

They peered through the crack in the door. Max activated his spy radar: pigtails bobbing, simpering smile, screeching voice. He knew what that meant. It was

Ben's sister, Enemy Agent Arabella Neal, codename: Manic Monitor.

"Enemy agent has window open," he whispered.

"Window open," repeated Ben, scribbling down the information. "She must have an evil plan to deafen everyone in Oldacre."

"I heard that!" snapped Arabella. She yanked open the door, and Max and Ben tumbled into the room. Arabella stomped off into the lounge.

"Plan failed, Agent Black," said Ben, picking himself up.

"We must try again," said Max, "this time in super silent mode."

Quick as cheetahs the boys scampered after her and ducked down behind the sofa.

Arabella was reading a magazine.

"Enemy agent scanning secret papers," reported Max.

"Scanning secret papers," repeated Ben as he scrawled down the words.

"Go away!" Arabella said grumpily.

She turned on the TV and started watching a programme about make-up. "That should get rid of them!" she muttered to herself.

Like shadows, the boys dived under the coffee table to get nearer.

"Plan working," hissed Ben. "She has
no idea we're here."

"Enemy agent studying cosmetics," said
Max. "She must be planning a dastardly
disguise."

"Dastardly disguise!" repeated Ben,
making notes. "She certainly needs it to
cover that ugly face."

"MUM!" shrieked Arabella. Mrs Neal
appeared at the door. "Max and Ben are
tormenting me."

"We were only spying on her," Ben
called from under the coffee table.

"Leave her alone," said his mother.

"I've got a job for you two."

"That doesn't sound like fun," whispered Max. "We're meant to be on half-term holiday."

Mrs Neal shooed them into the kitchen.

"You can make some fairy cakes for me while I do the housework."

The boys looked at her in disgust.

"Oozy mud cakes then," she said quickly. "Aprons on!"

"Mum!" gasped Ben in horror.

"All the top chefs wear aprons," said Mrs Neal, handing the boys two bright pinnies.

"Not covered in flowers, they don't," muttered Max.

He stopped when he saw Ben's mum produce a bowl of chocolate squares and put it over a pan on the cooker to melt. Then she picked up a duster and went off into the hall.

The boys sniffed the delicious smell of melting chocolate.

"What are we waiting for?" yelled Ben.

They read the recipe and began to measure out the ingredients. Max tossed the sugar into the mixing bowl – and all over the kitchen.

"Flour sifted!" said Ben, holding out a
bowl. "What's next?"

"Butter bomb!" Max announced. He
dropped the butter into the bowl, sending
a cloud of white flour into the air.

"Eggs surprise!" yelled Ben, splattering
the eggs into the mixture and then fishing
out the shells.

Max grabbed the whisk and began to
mix everything up into a gooey gloop.

Mrs Neal came in again. "Did you
have to make so much mess?" she
complained. She poured the melted
chocolate into the mixture. "Now stir this

in – carefully – while I find some paper cake cases." She went to rummage around in a cupboard.

Ben plunged his finger into the bowl and scooped a big blob of chocolatey goo into his mouth. "Just testing," he said.

"Me too," said Max, sticking a spoon in.

"Fantastic!" Ben took another helping.

"Yumtastic!" agreed Max, licking his lips and diving in again.

At last Mrs Neal appeared with the cake cases. She gawped into the bowl. "There's not enough left for even one cake!"

"We'd better finish it off then," said Ben helpfully.

"We wouldn't want it to go to waste," added Max.

Before Ben's mum could protest, the boys had scraped the bowl clean.

"We're off to play now," announced Ben.

"No you're not," said his mother crossly. "You're going to wash everything up. And I'll be back in a minute to check."

When she'd gone, Ben looked at the bowl. "This looks clean enough to put away," he said.

"You're right," agreed Max, licking the whisk in his hand. "None of it needs washing."

He began throwing spoons into the drawer.

"I can't hear water running!" they heard Mrs Neal shout from the hall.

"Better get on with it," groaned Ben.

Max ran warm water into the sink and added half a bottle of washing-up liquid. He looked at the mountain of bubbles spilling out. "This is the biggest ocean on Jupiter, and here comes an asteroid." He dropped the sieve into the foam.

"And some shooting stars," yelled Ben, pelting the bubbles with the spoons and whisk. Water splashed all over the counter – and the boys.

"Watch out for the crashing spaceship!" shouted Max, standing on a chair and dropping the bowl in. A huge wave washed out and soaked the floor.

"Boys!" Mrs Neal stood at the door, a look of horror on her face. "What have you done to my kitchen?"

"We're playing Alien Rocket Disaster," explained Ben patiently.

"I've had enough of your tricks," snapped his mother. "I'm phoning Mrs Black. You can go to Max's house for a while."

She grabbed the telephone off the wall. After a short conversation, she shepherded the boys to the door. "She's expecting you. Take your bikes and go straight there. We've decided that if you're not there in fifteen minutes you'll be grounded. You won't see each other for the rest of the week!"

Max and Ben looked at each other in horror, grabbed their bikes and rucksacks and shot off down the road.

"Secret plan alert, Agent Neal!" called Max. "Let's make a detour past the church and pick up the gargoylz. There should be time."

They arrived at St Mark's church, shot up the path and stopped by the porch with a squeal of brakes.

Max peered over at their school. "This is the best way to see Oldacre Primary," he said. "With the gates firmly locked and us on the outside!"

"Greetingz!" came a growly purr. "I've been looking out for you."

A monkey-faced gargoyle was peeping over the church porch at them.

"Hi, Toby!" called Max in delight.

"We would have been here sooner,"

explained Ben, "but there was a tidal wave in my kitchen."

"And we can't stop for long," said Max. "We'll be in big trouble if we don't get to my house soon."

Toby's face fell.

"But you can come with us," said Max, "and anyone else who's around."

Toby beamed. "Spluttering gutterz!" he said, using his secret power to fly down and join them. "I'd love to come."

A small snort of fire rose up from behind a headstone and a dragony gargoyle scrambled out. "And me!" he said. "As long as there are no tidal waves in your kitchen, Max. They might put my flames out."

"I don't think we'll be allowed near the sink, Azzan," said Ben. "Anyone else coming?"

"Me, please." Barney was right behind Azzan. The spines down his stony back quivered with excitement.

"Jump into our rucksacks then," Max told them. "We've got to be quick. My mum's expecting us in three minutes and we'll be grounded if we're late."

Pop! A grinning gargoyle appeared out of thin air, shaking his shaggy mane

happily. Zack's ability to become invisible was very useful when it came to playing tricks.

"Me too!" he yelled. "See you there!" **Pop!** He disappeared again.

The boys arrived at Max's house with seconds to spare. Mrs Black was waiting for them at the front door.

"You've just made it," she said sternly, checking her watch. "Now go and play quietly upstairs."

Max's rucksack wriggled. "We will!" came Toby's loud, growly voice.

"We're always quiet," added Azzan.

"Who said that?" asked Mrs Black, looking around.

"Well, it wasn't me or Ben," answered Max. "You must be hearing things, Mum!"

With that they bolted up the stairs.

"I can't think of any quiet games,"
said Ben when they were safely in Max's
bedroom.

"We could watch TV," said Toby.

"Or read comics," suggested Barney.

"I know a really quiet game," declared
Zack, jumping up excitedly. "Chase!
Catch me."

Pop! He disappeared, and the next
moment the bedroom door opened and
shut with a crash.

"Great!" said Azzan, bounding to the
door. "I love Chase."

Toby and Barney rushed after him.

Max blocked their way. "No," he cried. "Chase is far too noisy."

"And you might be seen by humans," added Ben. "We've got to stop Zack before he gets us into trouble."

"Whatever he does, Mum'll think it's us," said Max. "We'll be grounded for a year!"

The boys dashed out onto the landing and listened hard. Scampering footsteps could be heard going down the stairs.

"Quick!" yelled Max. "He's getting away."

They raced after Zack, pounding downstairs into the hall and running straight into Mrs Black, who was carrying a basket of washing. Vests and socks flew up into the air.

"You boys are horrendous!" exclaimed Mrs Black, struggling out from under the pile of clothes. She had a pair of pants stuck on her head. Max and Ben burst out laughing. Growly gargoyle chuckles rose up from under the shoe rack, where the boys could see the tips of three stony tails. The gargoylz had come down to see the fun. Then a dreadful pong filled the air.

"Uh-oh," whispered Ben. "Barney's got so excited he's let off a bottom burp!"

Barney's secret power was great, but sometimes his dreadful smells came out accidentally.

"This washing doesn't smell very clean," said Max quickly before his mum blamed them.

With a face like thunder, Mrs Black reached for the phone. "I'm calling Ben's mum to come and take him home," she said, pants slipping over her ears. "You two go out into the garden and stay there until she comes."

Max and Ben ran down to the trees at the bottom of the garden. They heard a swishing in the grass and saw that the gargoylz had joined them. They all rolled about laughing.

"Your mum looked so funny, Max!" chortled Azzan.

"Panty hat! Panty hat!" chanted Zack.

"I haven't laughed so much since we

ate the icing off the vicar's birthday cake and covered it in toothpaste instead," wheezed Toby, slapping his sides.

When the chuckles had died down at last, Zack held up a packet of biscuits. "Look what I found in the kitchen!" he said, sharing them out.

"Custard creamz!" sighed Barney. "My favourites."

Azzan blew a small flame in the air and held his biscuit up to it. "Breathing fire is a useful secret power," he announced, "Good for melting the custard."

"They were scrumptious!" exclaimed Zack when the packet was empty.

"Secret mission, Agent Neal," said Max. "Sneak into enemy headquarters – the kitchen – and get more supplies."

"I'm with you, Agent Black!" declared
Ben.

"We're coming too," Azzan told them.

"Last one there is a Jammy Dodger!"
shouted Ben, and he set off towards the
house, Max and the gargoylz close behind.

They slowed down to superspy
crawling speed as they got near the open
back door.

"Make sure the coast is clear," hissed
Max.

They crept forward and stopped dead
when they heard voices in the kitchen.

"They're driving
me mad!"

"Me too."

"That's our
mums," whispered Max.

"Are they talking about us?" asked Ben.

"Can't be!" Max inched forward
towards the back step. "They probably
mean Jessica and Arabella. My little sister
is the most annoying thing in the history
of most annoying things!"

They heard Max's mum sigh. "They're
only out of mischief when they're eating,"
she said. "And not always then."

"There's not enough food in the world
to keep them from causing trouble," put in
Mrs Neal.

"There's only one thing
for it," said Mrs Black
firmly. "We have to find
those boys a hobby."

Max and Ben looked

at each other in amazement. "They are talking about us!" gasped Max.

"They think we cause trouble!" said Ben in disbelief.

"Yoga's very calming," Mrs Black went on. "We might get a bit of peace and quiet if they do that."

"What's yoga?" demanded Toby. "Can you eat it?"

"It's something mums do," said Ben. "They stretch their legs and tie themselves in knots." He pulled a face.

"We've got to think of our own hobby," said Max, "and fast — before our mothers make us do yoga."

"Fire-breathing!" suggested Azzan. "Then we can practise together."

"That would be great," said Max,

"if we were dragons."

"You could learn to fly," put in Toby. "Then you'll be just like me."

"That would be great too," said Ben, "if we had wings."

"Disappearing!" Zack declared, popping in and out of sight.

"Well . . ." said Ben.

Max jumped up. "I've just remembered something awesome, Agent Neal. They've got kayaking classes on Oldacre Lake."

"Double awesome, Agent Black!" Ben punched the air. "And our mums might just agree! Come on . . ."

They bounded into the kitchen, making their mothers jump.

"We were just talking about finding you both a hobby," said Mrs Black. "There's a nice quiet embroidery class—"

"We'd like to go kayaking on Oldacre Lake!" burst in Max.

"I'm not sure about that," said Mrs Black. "Embroidery would be more likely to calm you down."

The boys were horrified.

"That's so girly, Mum!" gasped Max.

"We'd be sick all over our stitches," warned Ben.

Suddenly Max had a brilliant idea.

"I've changed my mind," he said. "It sounds lovely,"

"What!" Ben gaped at him in horror.

"Just think of it, Ben," Max went on, giving his friend a secret wink. "After sitting peacefully with our needles and thread, we'll be full of energy to play lots of pranks!"

Their mothers looked at each other in alarm.

"I suppose kayaking would tire them out," said Mrs Neal quickly.

"And it will keep them busy for a few hours," agreed Mrs Black. "We'll arrange it, boys."

Max and Ben jumped into their imaginary superspy canoes and rowed outside at turbo speed.

"We're going kayaking!" Ben told their waiting friends. "Come and watch."

The gargoylz jumped in the air with delight.

"This is going to be the most brilliant half-term ever!" exclaimed Max.

Castle Chaos

"I can't wait till we get to Barebones Castle," exclaimed Max Black. "It's going to be an awesome day out."

"And I can't wait for the medieval fight this afternoon," said his best friend, Ben Neal, peering out of the car window to catch his first glimpse of the castle. "It's knights on horses poking each other with long sticks!"

Ben's mum laughed. "It's called a joust," she told him. She was sitting in the front of the car, map reading for Mrs Black. Max and Ben were sitting in the folding seats at the very back with the picnic.

"You're so silly, Ben," his big sister, Arabella, piped up from the seat in front of them. "Fancy not knowing what a joust is."

"So silly," echoed Jessica, Max's five-year-old sister.

"Never mind the fighting," said Arabella. "What's more important is there'll be people in medieval costumes and they'll show us what life was like hundreds of years ago. It will be very interesting."

"Very interesting," chanted Jessica.

"There's only one thing spoiling today, Agent Neal," whispered Max. "Those two gruesome girls had to come with us."

"They should have stayed at home, Agent Black," agreed Ben. "Castles aren't for scaredy-cats like them. They're for superspies like us."

"And Jessica's always copying everything Arabella does," muttered Max. "She told Mum that when she's eleven she wants to be just like Arabella."

"But why does she have to start practising now?" groaned Ben.

"Look at her. She's got a pink hair band like Arabella . . ." said Max.

"And she giggles like Arabella," added Ben.

"And now she's even sniffing like Arabella," Max sighed.

"Two Arabellas," said Ben, pulling his hair in desperation.

"It's the worst nightmare in the history of worst nightmares."

"I hope our picnic's healthy," came Arabella's voice.

"I hope so too," said Jessica.

"I only eat healthy food," Arabella went on, "like vegetables."

"Ooh, I love vegetables," said Jessica.

"That's not true!" Max whispered to Ben. "Jess eats about one carrot a month – and then only if Mum makes her. If she had her way, she'd eat sweets for every meal."

But Ben wasn't listening. He was gawping at the plastic cool bag wedged between them.

"There's something alive in there," he gasped. "I saw the lid move."

Max peered at the bag.

"Maybe it's a snake," he said hopefully. "Or a rat."

He slowly opened the top.

"Greetingz!" came a growly purr, and a pair of golden eyes twinkled out of the darkness.

Max's spy radar burst into life: small, stone-coloured, and with a mischievous monkey face. Max knew what that meant. It was Toby, codename: Gargoyle Friend.

"Cool!" exclaimed Ben. "Who cares about stupid sisters when we've got Toby with us? This trip's going to be awesome after all!"

Toby and the other gargoylz lived on the church next to the boys' school. Everyone else thought they were just ugly

old statues but Max and Ben knew better.
The little stone creatures were alive and
loved to play tricks as much as the boys.

"Are we there yet?" came a chirpy
voice from the picnic basket at Ben's feet.

He flung it open. A gargoyle with
a long snout was sitting on the bags
of crisps.

"You're here too, Neb," whispered
Ben in delight.

"So's Barney,"
answered Neb in a
low voice. "He's busy
eating the cookiez."

"I've finished
them all!" A doggy
face appeared,
covered in crumbs.

It was Barney, wedged
between the muffins and
the jammy dodgers. "I'm so full I
can feel a smell coming on," he said.

"Don't do it in the car," gasped Toby. "Too pongy!"

Not only did the gargoylz like to play tricks, they all had their own special powers as well. Barney could make the most amazing bottom-burp smells. The problem was, he couldn't always control them!

Max peered into the cool bag. "I hope no one's had the sausage rolls," he said. "They're my favourite."

He had just picked up a handful of sandwiches to check underneath, when Arabella's face appeared between the headrests. Jessica popped up next to her.

Neb used his special power to change colour so that he blended into the background like a chameleon, and Toby and Barney hid under the seats.

"Are you starting on the picnic?" demanded Arabella.

"How naughty!" Jessica piped up.

"You've eaten all the cookies!" snapped Arabella, peering into the basket.

"Every single one!" gasped Jessica.

"*We* didn't eat them," protested Max.

"Yes we did," said Ben quickly. He nudged Max. "We can't tell them who really ate them!" he muttered.

"Er . . . OK, yes, we did eat them," stammered Max.

"Greedy boys," said Arabella. "I'm telling Mum."

"So am I," added Jessica.

"But you said you

were only going to eat healthy food," said Ben, "so you wouldn't have wanted any cookies anyway!"

Arabella glared at them. Then she sniffed and turned away. Jessica did the same. "OK, I'll let you off this time," Arabella said over her shoulder.

"Clever answer, Agent Neal," whispered Max.

Toby and Barney crept out from their hiding places, and Neb stopped looking like the picnic basket and changed back to his usual stony colour.

"Sorry," said Barney sheepishly. "I didn't mean to eat all the cookiez. They just sort of jumped into my mouth."

At that moment the car swung round a corner and the castle came into view. It was huge, with four tall turrets and long red and gold banners hanging down from the battlements.

Toby pressed his nose against the window. "It's much bigger than Saint Mark's Church," he said, eyes wide with amazement.

"You'll love it, gargoylz," Max told them. "There are knights and a moat – and even a torture chamber."

"They used to have torture chambers when we were young," said Barney nervously. "Nasty places."

"That was hundreds of years ago," Ben assured him. "They don't use them any more. It's just a really cool bunch of gory pokers and thumbscrews and all that sort of thing."

"Can't wait!" declared Neb in excitement.

"We've got a problem, though," said Max, scratching his head. "How do we get the gargoylz out of the car without anyone seeing them?"

"Got it!" said Ben. "Secret plan: Distract Everyone."

"Brilliant!" answered Max. "Then the gargoylz can make their getaway!"

"Now it is time for one of my smellz!" said Barney. "No one will stay in the car after that!"

Max and Ben made a face at each other. "We'll have to use our superspy nose clamps," said Max. "Codename: Fingers."

The car pulled into a parking space. Barney's eyes glazed over and the next second a dreadful pong filled the air. It was like the smelliest rotten eggs in the world. Max and Ben pinched their noses hard.

"Oh, boys!" groaned Ben's mum, flinging open the door.

"Everyone out!" gasped Max's mum. She handed Max the keys. "Once that smell has gone from my car, lock up and come and join us."

"Stinkpots!" said Arabella, diving out of the car and making for the castle entrance.

"Stinky stinkpots!" shrieked Jessica, close behind her.

As soon as they'd all gone, Ben opened his door to let the gargoylz out. "Good trick!" he spluttered, flapping the smell away with a paper plate.

"See you later!" whispered Toby. He and Neb scuttled off into the bushes.

"One more gargoyle to go," called Barney mysteriously as he scampered after the others.

"One more?" said Max, looking around in amazement. "I can't see anyone else."

They searched among the picnic things.

"Barney must have been tricking us," said Ben, pulling out a rolled-up picnic blanket and flopping down on it. "There are no other gargoylz here."

To his surprise the blanket snorted! Ben shot to his feet. The boys quickly pulled at the corners, unrolling the blanket, and a lumpy, troll-like gargoyle fell out.

"Rufus!" exclaimed Ben. "That blanket was a mega-good hiding place!"

"And it kept Barney's smell away," said Rufus, sitting up dizzily.

He got to his feet and staggered after his friends,

a cheeky grin on his huge, warty face.

"Secret plan successful!" declared Max.

"Castle, here we come!" yelled Ben.

They bounded across the drawbridge over the moat. Their mums were buying tickets from a man dressed like an olden days guard.

"This castle is so cool!" said Ben, examining the map on the wall. "Where shall we go first? The torture chamber or the battlements?"

"Queen's bedchamber!" said Arabella firmly.

"Queen's bedchamber," repeated Jessica-the-Echo. "There might be some pretty princess clothes there."

"And we'll all go together," said Ben's mum, paying the cashier. "We can't trust you two boys to behave on your own after that nasty smelly trick."

Max and Ben groaned as they trailed up the main staircase.

"Why would anyone want to look

at clothes when there are instruments of torture to play with?" whispered Max. "Mothers are as bad as girls sometimes."

Arabella let out a shriek of delight when she saw the long robes displayed on models around the royal four-poster bed. Jessica cried out too.

A woman in medieval costume came forward and curtsied. She pointed to a long rack of brightly coloured clothes.

"I am your humble servant, young mistresses," she said. "Allow me to help you dress up."

The girls shrieked again.

The boys gawped at each other. "Get back against the wall," said Ben quickly. "We don't want to get dressed up!"

"Look at me!" trilled Jessica as the servant put a tall pointy hat with a long flowing veil on her head.

Once she'd helped both Jessica and Arabella dress like medieval princesses, the servant curtsied again. "I will leave you now, my ladies. I have others to attend to," she said, and left the room.

The mums cooed and took
photographs as Arabella paraded around
the room in a trailing gown, with Jessica
following behind in her princess hat
and velvet cloak.

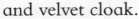

The boys
slumped in a
corner.

"This is
so boring!"
moaned Max.
"There's not
even a suit of
armour to try on. How do we
escape, Agent Neal?"

To his surprise Ben was grinning. "Help
is at hand, Agent Black," he whispered.

Max heard Toby's growly chuckle
coming from the costume rack. The next
minute a long red dress began to jiggle
on its hanger! Luckily Mrs Black and
Mrs Neal were too busy examining their

photos of the girls to notice.

The boys watched eagerly as Arabella swept over to change outfits, followed by her faithful shadow, Jessica. The red dress suddenly flapped a sleeve under their noses. The two girls screamed in horror and ran off to hide behind the bed. Then a glove rose up from the shelf and waved at them. The boys could just see the outline of Neb with the glove on the end of his nose. They heard Barney doing his best ghostly wail from the hat stand.

"There are ghosts in the clothes!" squealed Arabella.

"Ghosts!" echoed Jessica in terror.

Max and Ben stuffed their fists in their

mouths to stop themselves snorting with laughter.

"You're imagining things!" declared Max's mum, steering the trembling girls out of the room. "Clothes can't be haunted!"

"Was that another of your tricks, boys?" asked Mrs Neal suspiciously.

"Not us," said Max as they followed them into the corridor. "We were miles away."

Arabella glanced fearfully back over her shoulder.

So did Jessica.

A pair of shoes began to tap dance on the floor. A white petticoat was bouncing around them, followed by a lacy blouse, two hats and a pair of bloomers.

The girls shrieked, and scuttled off down the staircase. Max and Ben caught up with them at the bottom.

"I wouldn't go near that room again, girls," advised Max, trying to keep a straight face.

"The gruesome ghosts of the wardrobe live there," warned Ben. "You might feel a shiver in your shirt."

"Or a spook in your skirt," said Max.

"Or a phantom in your pants," added Ben helpfully.

"We'll go to the kitchen instead," quavered Arabella.

"Pots and pans aren't haunted," said Jessica.

"Good idea," said Ben's mum in relief.

Max and Ben groaned. "Do we have to come?" Ben asked. "We want to go to the dungeon. It's more fun than stupid cooking."

"We were good in the queen's bedchamber," Max pointed out.

"All right then," said his mum. "But make sure you behave yourselves."

"*Us*?" said Max, looking shocked.

"We always behave ourselves," said Ben.

Before their mothers could reply, they raced off down the stone steps that led to the dungeon.

"This is so cool!" exclaimed Max as they wandered among the rusty old pliers and thumbscrews in the gloomy torture chamber. Grim-looking models stood around holding chains and spikes, and the ancient walls were lit by lamps that looked like flickering candles. Every so often blobs of red slime slid down the walls.

"It looks just like blood," gasped Ben.
"I hope the gargoylz get here soon. They'll
love it."

"Here's the rack!" said Max eagerly. He
led the way to a huge wooden frame with
a ragged figure tied to it by his hands and
feet. "I bet those medieval people ended up
really tall after they'd been stretched
on here. They'd have been really good
at basketball."

"What's this?" asked Ben, stopping at
a long metal cabinet that was standing
against a wall. "It looks like the sort of
case you'd find an Egyptian mummy in."
Max read the label. *"Iron Maiden.*

Prisoners were shut in here and spiked to death."

"Gruesome!" said Ben, fiddling with the lock. "Let's open it. There might still be someone full of holes inside."

"Shouldn't think so," Max began. "No one gets spiked nowadays—"

Ben flung open the case and the boys jumped back in astonishment. The iron maiden wasn't empty! A stone-coloured, warty creature was standing inside, grinning at them.

"Rufus!" gasped Ben. "What are you doing in there?"

"I was having a doze," Rufus answered with a grin.

"Don't the spikes hurt?" asked Max.

Rufus shook his head. "I'm smaller than humanz – too small for the spikes to reach me,"

he assured them.

Just then they heard the ghastly chatter of girly voices.

"It's our sisters!" groaned Max. "So our mums won't be far behind."

"They're coming this way," added Ben urgently. "They'll see Rufus!"

Max swung the heavy case shut just as the girls appeared, he and Ben hurriedly stood in front of it.

"Mum says you have to meet us outside for the picnic in one hour," said Arabella, giving a shiver as she glanced around.

"One hour precisely," added Jessica, wagging her finger.

"See you later then," said Max, trying to shoo them away.

Arabella peered hard at the boys. "You look

guilty," she said suspiciously. "What have you been up to?"

"Nothing," said Ben, putting on his wide-eyed, innocent look. It always worked with the dinner ladies at school, who gave him extra waffles. It *never* worked with his sister.

"What's that thing behind you?" she demanded.

"We want to know!" insisted Jessica, trying to push past.

"It's a nasty iron maiden," Max said desperately. He had to stop them seeing Rufus. "You wouldn't like it."

"Oh yes we would," said Arabella. "An iron maiden doesn't sound nasty at all."

"It is," said Ben. "Honest."

Arabella snorted.

"I don't believe you. Get out of the way."

"Yes, get out of the way!" said Jessica-the-Echo.

Max and Ben held their breath as Arabella heaved the metal case open. The door swung back with a clang – revealing a pale, grinning skeleton!

It lolled in the iron maiden with long, dangling limbs and dead eyes that stared straight at the girls. Rufus had used his special power and had turned into a terrifying pile of bones.

Arabella let out an ear-splitting shriek that bounced around the walls of the dungeon. So did Jessica. Max and Ben clapped their hands over their ears. The girls turned and collided with their mothers. They screeched again and fled up the stone staircase.

"It wasn't us," Max called to his mum. "They just saw a silly skeleton."

"We did tell them not to look, Agent Black," said Ben sympathetically as their mums disappeared after the girls.

"It's not our fault they didn't listen, Agent Neal," agreed Max, shaking his head. "Well done, Rufus!"

Rufus stepped out of the iron maiden and took a bow. "That was my best

performance yet!" he declared as he
shrank back into his stony form.

The other gargoylz came scuttling out
from behind a metal cage.

"We saw it all," said Barney.

"I haven't laughed so much since Neb
sniffed up a bunch of grapes and pelted
the vicar with pips," chuckled Toby.

Ben rubbed his hands together. "Now
our scaredy-cat sisters have gone, we've
got the whole castle to explore."

"What are we waiting for?" cried Max.
"Let's have a medieval spy adventure!"

WORDSEARCH

Another super-spy search for words!
There are 10 to find ... can you find the
bonus word that isn't listed below?

F	A	I	R	G	R	O	U	N	D	L	B	Y
M	T	P	L	E	I	J	N	B	U	M	O	B
S	U	P	E	R	S	P	Y	T	A	V	U	F
S	K	Z	S	M	P	E	S	O	O	H	N	J
B	P	A	F	U	B	A	R	N	E	Y	C	H
I	B	L	T	B	U	Q	P	C	H	M	Y	Q
J	S	K	U	E	B	U	D	N	T	U	C	W
A	A	L	L	E	B	A	R	A	D	E	A	Y
A	S	T	L	U	E	O	O	F	V	S	S	V
U	K	I	X	N	U	T	A	S	T	U	T	C
S	X	I	U	G	U	J	I	R	U	M	L	R
F	O	Q	J	R	R	E	A	L	D	H	E	G
Z	M	A	E	R	C	D	R	A	T	S	U	C

Words:

Bouncy Castle   museum
skateboard   fairground
superspy   Arabella
Eli   Theo
Custard Creamz   ???????

Solutions

Page 30

U	T	M	D	S	Y	F	R	C	T	W	Y
A	G	P	O	N	L	B	F	R	Z	J	D
T	U	A	Z	U	J	O	O	S	N	A	O
C	H	U	R	C	H	T	O	T	E	V	P
C	L	M	O	G	C	B	T	O	B	N	N
L	N	O	T	S	O	A	B	W	U	G	O
I	O	F	N	J	E	Y	A	B	L	E	I
C	G	X	O	B	W	L	L	Y	B	P	S
O	L	D	A	C	R	E	L	E	T	C	S
H	A	V	S	M	P	O	W	J	B	V	I
S	T	O	O	B	Y	S	S	O	B	O	M
Z	L	V	K	X	K	A	V	B	G	O	F

Page 98

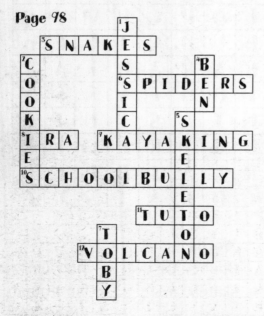

Page 188

MEET US AT THE BACK OF THE SPORTS FIELD NEAR THE HEDGE.
BART HAS A NEW JOKE!

Solutions

Page 132

WE ARE HAVING A SLEEP-OVER IN THE GARDEN TONIGHT.
BRING ALL THE GARGOYLZ!

Page 158

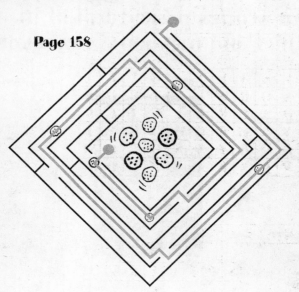

Page 282

BARNEY

BART

THEO

ZACK

AZZAN

ELI

CYRUS

RUFUS

Page 314

F	A	I	R	G	R	O	U	N	D	I	B	Y
M	T	P	L	E	I	J	N	B	U	M	O	B
S	U	P	E	R	S	P	Y	T	A	V	U	F
S	K	Z	S	M	P	E	S	O	O	H	N	J
B	P	A	F	U	B	A	R	N	E	Y	C	H
I	B	L	T	B	U	Q	P	C	H	M	Y	Q
J	S	K	U	E	B	U	D	N	T	U	C	W
A	A	L	L	E	B	A	R	A	D	E	A	Y
A	S	T	L	U	E	O	O	F	V	S	S	V
U	K	I	X	N	U	T	A	S	T	U	T	C
S	X	I	U	G	U	J	I	R	U	M	L	R
F	O	O	J	R	R	E	A	L	D	H	E	G
Z	M	A	E	R	C	D	R	A	T	S	U	C

COLLECT ALL THE GARGOYLZ TITLES

Four stories packed full of magic, mischief and mayhem in every book!